The bulb flicked on. And in the mirror I saw what might have been a face, dim and unfocused, hovering slightly above my left shoulder. I felt the hairs on the back of my neck fizz. I blinked. But the shape remained where it had been, smudgy and undefined. Just that. Just a shape like a face, with dark spaces that could be eyes, a line of nose, a shadow of mouth.

I felt a chill in the pit of my stomach. "Dumb," I whispered out loud. "It's nothing but an old smudgy mirror. There's nothing there."

Before I could turn again, the two lightbulbs, both at the same moment, flared blue and burned out, leaving a scent of hot dust in the darkness.

The Face in the Mirror

Stephanie S. Tolan

HarperTrophy®
An Imprint of HarperCollinsPublishers

The Face in the Mirror
Copyright © 1998 by Stephanie S. Tolan
All rights reserved. No part of this book may be used or reproduced in any manner
whatsoever without written permission except in the case of brief quotations embodied
in critical articles and reviews. Printed in the United States of America. For information
address HarperCollins Children's Books, a division of HarperCollins Publishers,
1350 Avenue of the Americas, New York, NY 10019.

Library of Congress Cataloging-in-Publication Data
Tolan, Stephanie S.
    The face in the mirror / Stephanie S. Tolan.
      p.   cm.
    Summary: Joining his estranged father in a professional production of Shakespeare's
"Richard III," Jared tries to cope with acting insecurities, his obnoxious half brother,
and a theatre ghost.
    ISBN 0-688-15394-1 — ISBN 0-380-73263-7 (pbk.)
    [1. Theatre—Fiction.   2. Ghosts—Fiction.   3. Brothers—Fiction.]   I. Title.
PZ7.T5735Fac   1998   97-48359
[Fic]—dc21   CIP
                                                                                          AC

First Harper Trophy edition, 2000

Visit us on the World Wide Web!
www.harperchildrens.com

For my theatre family:
Bob, who brought the history of "the western
stage" and all those old theatres into my life,
and RJ, whose passion for Shakespeare inspired the
Star Wars Richard

...and for the ghost at the Fulton Opera House

CHAPTER
ONE

"Now is the winter of our discontent/Made glorious summer...."

That's how Shakespeare's *The Tragedy of King Richard the Third* begins. It's a play I knew pretty well by June the year my grandfather had his stroke. The "winter of our discontent" was not a bad description of the winter I'd just had, so as I got off the bus in Addison, Michigan, that hot, humid day with the acting script in one hand and my duffel in the other, I was doing my best to hope that "glorious summer" would fit the next couple of months.

Pop was still in the nursing home, working every day with a physical therapist (a big guy he called the "physical terrorist") to try to get the left side of his body working again, and Serena had gone back to New York City. She'd skipped out the very minute she could, not even hanging around long enough to get me to the bus station that morning—Pop's old chess buddy, Mr. Steinmetz, had done that.

Serena, who is blond and beautiful and baby-faced, is still playing ingenues. That's just as well. As good an actress as she claims to be, nobody would ever believe her playing a mother. Pop—her dad—took over that part in my life when I was two. That's when she dumped her last name, Krebbs—and me—and went off to be a Broadway star. The idea was that as soon as she made it big, she'd come back to Cincinnati and get me. Only she never made it quite big enough for that.

I'd read *Richard III* (as it's usually called) on the bus for what must have been the tenth time. In the last month, I'd also watched videos of the old movie with Laurence Olivier and one with Ian McKellen, and a movie with Al Pacino about doing *Richard III*. This wasn't because I had any great passion for Shakespeare. I'd never read a single thing of his before. It was because Pop was determined that I was going to be just what he is—a survivor. And Shakespeare, starting with *Richard*, was going to be the admission ticket to the summer, and just maybe the whole rest of my life.

Pop calls this "ironic." He's a real theatre buff. Before the stroke dumped him in the hospital, and then in the nursing home, he went as often as he could afford to—there's a lot of theatre in Cincinnati. He always offered to take me along, but

I wouldn't go. I hated the theatre. As far as I was concerned, the only thing it had ever done for me was steal my mother. Now it was about to take over everything.

The reason I had come to Addison, Michigan, was that the New World Shakespeare Company was there, and so was its producer/director, Phillip Kingsley. My father. A man I'd never seen—or even heard of—until Pop had the stroke and Serena came back to Cincinnati to say that she still couldn't (or wouldn't) take me to live with her in New York.

I always thought she'd just made up my name, Jared Kingsley, because she hated the name Krebbs. But Pop had known the truth all along. The stroke paralyzed the whole left side of his body, but he could still think and talk and use the telephone, so he managed to track Phillip Kingsley down. The man had been a stage actor when Serena knew him, but he'd done some directing, too. Then, for nearly ten years, he'd made movies. Now he'd left Hollywood and was starting a Shakespeare company in the newly renovated, historic Addison Opera House. The first show was to be *Richard III*, and he was playing the part of Richard as well as directing it.

There are two princes in the play, and when Pop found him, Phillip Kingsley still needed a kid actor to play one of them, so I was going to get a father, a place to live for however long I needed one, and a job, all at once. "No sweat," Pop told me when I said

I didn't want to act and, anyway, I didn't know how. "Whatever you have to do, you *can* do." And anyway, he reminded me, the part wasn't all that big or Phillip Kingsley wouldn't have taken a chance on me sight unseen.

I had gotten my first look at the guy out the window of the bus as it pulled up to the curb in front of the drugstore that is the closest thing Addison, Michigan, has to a bus station. He was dressed in a sort of creamy white color, shoes and socks and slacks and an open shirt that showed off his tan. Long wavy hair, brown, with a touch of gray at the temples, surrounded his face like a lion's mane. He was leaning against the hood of a black Saab convertible with California plates. People on the street turned to look at Phillip Kingsley just the way people always turned to look at Serena, and I could tell that, like Serena, he was aware of every single glance. He had a smile pasted firmly on his face, and when I came down the steps, he held out a smooth, long-fingered hand to shake mine.

After we got my stuff into the car, Phillip Kingsley drove around Addison, showing it off. To me, it just looked like a grubby little farm town pretending to be something else. But he acted like it was some kind of national treasure. It had a couple of seedy-looking strip malls, one with a two-screen movie theatre playing movies that were already at the cheap flicks at home. It also had a historical section, all freshly painted houses and restored build-

4

ings and gift shops and galleries with wooden signs whose lettering was carved and done with gold leaf. He said that was what made it so special, so right for what he wanted to do here. That, and the fact that it's between Toledo and Detroit, so audiences could come from two big cities.

I did my best to look at Addison instead of at this man who was my father. But I couldn't help it: I kept looking for something in his face that I recognized from looking in a mirror. The nose maybe. Or the eyebrows. For sure the cleft in his chin. He kept glancing at me as he talked, probably doing exactly the same thing. I'd look away when he did it, but finally our eyes met and I got embarrassed, so I stayed focused on the sights he was pointing out after that.

We couldn't drive past the theatre, because it was down a cobblestoned street that was closed to traffic. The street was lined with old-fashioned gas street-lamps and bright banners. "The historical society did a beautiful job renovating the theatre—with help from the college." Phillip Kingsley sounded as proud as if he'd built the place single-handedly. I could see only a bit of the marquee, and I wasn't all that impressed. It didn't look that much different from any old downtown movie theatre. Phillip Kingsley went on talking about nineteenth-century opera houses and how important classical theatre was, especially Shakespeare. I had quit listening. Pop! I thought. What'm I going to do here?

Pop's voice was as clear in my head as if he were sitting in the seat between me and Phillip Kingsley. *Survive, guy. Survive!*

Finally, we got to a huge shabby three-story gray frame house. There was a big yellow dog in the backyard, chained to a doghouse. He was lying in the shade under a tree, and he wagged his tail when we drove up, but he didn't bark or get up. "Most of the acting company lives here," Phillip Kingsley said. "It makes food and transportation easier and saves a bundle on rent."

He turned off the car's engine and sat for a minute, looking at his hands on the steering wheel. I glanced down at my own hands—another resemblance. Then he turned to look at me, face-on, more directly than he had since he'd shaken my hand. His eyes were brown, like mine, but darker. "I want you to know that I never knew about you. I really didn't. Serena never told me."

I didn't know what to say, so I just nodded. That made two of us.

"Just so you know." And then he got out and I followed.

As we carried my stuff past the dog, me with my big duffel and Phillip Kingsley with my boxes, he wagged some more, but he still didn't get up. He looked like he was used to being ignored and didn't seem to mind.

In the huge kitchen of the house, a round, balding guy wearing shorts and an undershirt covered by

6

a stained white apron was stirring a batch of red sauce on a great big old black-and-white gas stove. Phillip Kingsley introduced him as Del—"the finest Falstaff of his generation. Plays Buckingham in *Richard*, and tonight—our chef." I didn't know what a Falstaff was, but I figured from the garlicky smell of the sauce that the guy was a decent chef.

"Delvechio at your service," the man boomed, sauce dripping from the wooden spoon he waved as he talked. "Tonight we have cavatini Delvechio, a dish I created myself." He kissed the fingers of his free hand. "Fit for a king"—he grinned at Phillip Kingsley—"or a long-lost prince!"

It wasn't *me* who'd been lost, I thought, but I nodded and the man went back to stirring.

Phillip Kingsley took me upstairs then, to the room I was to share with his other son, my half brother, Theodore. Called Tad. This was the wrinkle of this new life that Pop thought was best of all. "Think of it," he'd said. "You've got a brother! You always wanted a brother."

That was only partly right. What I'd wanted when I was little was an *older* brother. A bigger one. Somebody to protect me when the guys in the neighborhood beat up on me, which happened a lot. Pop got me karate lessons, and by the time I'd made brown belt, I could hold my own with any of them. After that, I quit thinking about a brother. But I didn't correct Pop when he said it. He was putting up a good front, but I knew he was upset that he was having to send me away. I figured I could put up a good front, too.

But the minute Phillip Kingsley pulled open the bedroom door, my heart sank. The room looked like it had been hit by a tornado. Except for a brand-new futon against the far wall that was apparently supposed to be my bed, the place was ankle-deep in socks and dirty underwear, shirts and pants and shoes, stuffed animals, books, papers, action figures, trucks and tanks and airplanes. It was a slob's room. A *childish* slob's room. Tad was supposed to be almost thirteen, only a little over a year younger than me. I'd outgrown stuff like this ages ago.

"Sorry it's such a mess. Tad was supposed to clean up today, but he doesn't seem to have gotten to it." Phillip Kingsley set down the boxes of mine he was carrying—outside the door, the only place where there was enough floor space for them. "Tad's always had a room to himself."

"Me too."

"Then you'll both have some adapting to do," he said. "We'll get some boundaries established, and I'm sure it won't be too difficult. I think you're going to find it's a great thing to have a brother, once you get used to it." He looked around the room for a moment and shook his head. "Maybe you'll be a good influence."

It would take a bulldozer to have any kind of influence on this mess, I thought.

"All right." Phillip Kingsley clapped me on the

8

back. "I'll give you a tour of the theatre after dinner. I'd like you to sit in tonight to get a feel for things. We've been in rehearsal for a week, but you don't have to worry about catching up. Your scenes are pretty small, and we won't be blocking them for a while yet." I took a step or two into the room, trying not to step on anything breakable. "Everyone will be back here at about five-thirty. Till then, you can put your clothes away—that's your dresser over there— and make yourself at home. I'm off to stage combat class right now—fencing. You can start that on Tuesday. I'm sure you'll like it. Tad does."

I nodded. Something else I'd never done in my life. *Whatever you have to do, you* can *do.*

"See you later." And Phillip Kingsley hurried off and left me to try to figure out where to put my stuff.

I unpacked my duffel, putting my clothes into the dresser near my futon and shoving the duffel into the closet. It was a good thing I didn't have anything that needed a hanger, because the closet rod was jammed full of Tad's shirts and slacks and jackets. The kid had more dress clothes than Pop and I owned between us. I dragged my boxes in from the hall, shoving toys and clothes out of the way, but I didn't bother to open them. I just left them stacked at the foot of my bed. There was no place to put anything.

I kicked off my shoes and lay facedown on the dark cover of the futon, trying to will myself to go to sleep. I hadn't slept much the night before. But it didn't work. It occurred to me suddenly that Phillip Kingsley hadn't asked me a single question about my life. You'd think a father who'd just met a son he never knew he had would want to know at least a little something about him.

I turned on my back and found myself looking at a framed poster on the wall by the door. It was an advertisement for baby food, showing a smiling, dimpled toddler wearing nothing but a diaper and a beet-stained grin. It had to be Tad. The kid had done commercials all his life, even before he'd gotten a bunch of small parts in movies and a big part in a soap opera. This was my new brother, who was going to play the other prince in *Richard III*—a kid who'd been acting since he was in diapers.

There's no knowing what cards life's going to deal you. Pop had said that so often, it had worn a groove in my brain. *The only thing that matters is how you play 'em.*

"But this isn't fair," I said out loud. "It's like finding a jack of lemons in with the hearts and spades."

I wanted to call him, to hear his voice for real, but there wasn't a phone in his room in the nursing home. He had to get wheeled out into the lobby to use the phone, and the last time I'd visited, he told me not to expect a call for a while. He wanted me to get settled in first, get to know my new family. Anyway, I knew exactly what he'd say: *Who ever told you life was fair?*

I must have slept then, because I woke up when the dog started barking outside. A car door slammed. Voices. I got up, ran a hand through my hair, and stuffed my bare feet into my sneakers. I smoothed the dark blue cover of the futon and fluffed the pillow. I'm not exactly the neatest person in the whole world, but I'm no slob. Then, kicking a pathway through the clutter as I went, I headed downstairs.

CHAPTER
TWO

The kitchen, big as it was, seemed crowded now. Del was still at the stove, and I counted five guys all wearing white, high-collared fencing jackets, all talking at once, having some kind of argument. In the center was a tall, skinny man with thinning mousy brown hair and ears that stuck out from his head like car doors. I could only catch little bits of what they were saying.

"...calling him a liar?"

"...superstition. Plain superstition..."

"If you'd been to England, you'd believe..."

"You've been listening to too many of Joan's stories...."

The tall one's voice silenced everybody else. "I tell you, I know what I saw. And I know what I felt!"

"Oh, George, don't be so dramatic." A short

young woman with a cloud of curly blond hair pushed her way through the group and came toward the stove. She was dressed in a tank top and baggy cutoff overalls. "Tell 'em, Del. If there is a ghost, it's a *theatre* ghost! Theatre ghosts are always good ones, aren't they? They bring luck."

"So they say." Del went back to pushing something around in a huge frying pan.

Ghosts. These people, these adult human beings, were actually arguing about a ghost! Nutcases, I thought. Every one of them.

The blond turned back to George then. He towered over her, but she faced him with her hands on her hips. "There's no point arguing about it. Either there is or there isn't one. If there is, we're bound to find out."

"There *is* one, all right, Toni," George said. "And you'll change your tune when you meet up with it."

Before Toni could answer, the back door opened and the dog, all energy suddenly, bounded through, barking and leaping, his tail wagging frantically. The guys all tried to protect their white jackets from his huge dusty paws. "Whoa, Hamlet...."

"Down, boy."

"Look out!"

"Tad!" George yelled. "Get this brute out of here!"

As the other guys moved out of the way of the leaping dog, I saw across the room a pudgy boy in a stained and rumpled fencing jacket. His brown hair was stuck to his forehead with sweat and he was chewing gum, popping it noisily. Over one shoulder, he had a shiny black fencing bag almost as big as he was, and he was trying to get it loose from where it had caught on the screen door as he came through.

"Hamlet's got as much right inside as anybody," he said in a whiny voice that cracked and changed pitch. He kicked the door, and the bag came loose, throwing him into the room. "How'd *you* like to be stuck on the end of a chain in the yard all day long?"

Suddenly, the dog noticed me. He came at me, his huge paws catching me in the chest and knocking me backward into the wall. Making little yelping noises, he slathered my face with his tongue.

"Down, Hamlet!" Phillip Kingsley's voice dropped him like a cannonball. The dog flattened himself against the floor and lay there, his tail thumping steadily. I stood up and wiped my cheek on my T-shirt sleeve.

Phillip Kingsley, in a blindingly white fencing jacket with P.K. embroidered over his heart in red, stood in the doorway behind Tad. "Everyone, I'd like you to meet my son Jared. Jared"—he swept his hand around the room, calling the names in order—"George Beattie, Toni Webster, Kent Zeller, Laurence Howard—our fencing coach—Sam Krieger, Dennis Young—you've met Del—and"—he put his other hand on the head of the kid in front of him—"this is your half brother, Tad. Jared, Prince of Wales, meet Tad, Duke of York."

14

The fencing bag slid off Tad's shoulder with a thump. He looked at me, his eyes squinted and his nose wrinkled.

I nodded. "Hi."

He snapped his gum. "Hello," he said, in a tone that made me think, if he were younger, he'd have stuck out his tongue.

Phillip Kingsley made Tad put Hamlet back outside and then sent him up to change. The fencers went, too. I stayed in the kitchen, where Del was tearing lettuce into a gigantic salad bowl and Toni was setting the table.

I offered to help Toni. She said she'd be glad to have help, but I really ought to take advantage of its being my first day. "By tomorrow, they'll have you up on the assignment sheet like everybody else. Voluntary, of course." She pointed to a bulletin board by the back door. "If a mouse showed his nose around here, it would get put on crumb detail. Even Tad has a job."

She ran a hand through her blond curls, fluffing them up even more. "I'm the stage manager. Someday, though, I hope to be the ingenue. You know what an ingenue is?" I just nodded. She fit the definition better than Serena, agewise, even if she wasn't as pretty.

She rummaged through a drawer and flung a double handful of silverware on the table. "Put these out, would you?"

An actor cooking and a stage manager setting the table. It wasn't exactly what I'd expected. But then, I hadn't known what to expect. The silverware, some of it dented and bent, looked as if it might have been snatched, a spoon or fork at a time, from assorted truck stops and diners. Toni talked steadily, about how she'd met Phillip and Julia, how excited she was to be in a Shakespeare company, how Shakespeare was the greatest playwright who'd ever lived or ever would live. I only half listened.

"Did George say he'd seen a ghost?" I asked when she finally stopped to catch her breath.

She raised her eyebrows. "You heard that, huh?"

"You don't believe it, do you?"

Toni shrugged. "Lots of old theatres have ghosts. No reason the Addison Opera House couldn't have one, too."

"But—"

"Could be just George messing with people's heads."

"There's no such thing as a ghost," I told her.

"Well, whatever. Just don't mention ghosts around Tad. Phillip and Julia are pretty protective of that kid." She set a stack of mismatched plates on the table and motioned for me to set them out. "They had to work hard to protect him out in Hollywood—you know, from the whole L.A. scene—fast kids and druggies and all. Which is why she wouldn't let him go to school out there. When he wasn't getting tutored on a set, he had tutors at home. He's spent his whole life with adults. Even in his movies, even in the soap, he was always the only kid. It'll be good for him to have another kid around."

It hadn't looked to me as if Tad wanted another kid around.

Toni changed the subject then and went on chattering. I was pouring water into the glasses she had put out when the back door opened and a broad woman with a mass of white hair piled on top of her head bustled in. She waved a knitting bag at Toni. "Antoinette, you've left the van in Julia's place—again!" She had an English accent that made her sound like something out of *Masterpiece Theatre*.

Toni dropped a package of paper napkins onto the table. "Rats! I forgot to move it."

I had gone back to pouring water when the screen door creaked open again behind me.

"Sorry, Julia," Toni said. "I'll move both of them, if you'll just—"

I turned and set the water pitcher on the table with a bang that sloshed water all over the tablecloth.

Julia Kingsley—my stepmother—was the most beautiful woman I had ever seen. She made Serena's blond roundness seem almost ordinary. Like the difference between a Barbie doll and a Greek statue. She was very tall, almost as tall as Phillip, I was pretty sure, and slim. Her skin was a soft, creamy golden tan, and her hair was dark red and thick and wavy. She was dressed in a long green skirt with a top that was like a scarf or a cape—a swirl of bright greens and blues and purples. And she was looking at me so intently, I could feel my ears getting hot.

"You must be Jared," she said, and her voice was like warm honey. "I'm Julia Kingsley." She touched the shoulder of the woman in front of her. "Joan Latimer, may I present Jared Kingsley, Phillip's older son. He'll be playing the Prince of Wales. Joan is playing Phillip's mother, the Duchess of York."

"Your Highness," Joan Latimer said with a solemn curtsy that made my ears even hotter. "Terribly pleased to make your acquaintance!" She winked then, and grinned as she held out her hand to shake mine. "How do you do?"

"Uh...very well, thank you," I managed to say, even though I was having trouble getting my breath.

"He's a stunner, this one!" Joan Latimer said to Julia Kingsley.

I was suddenly aware of my old cutoffs, my ratty sneakers, my faded T-shirt. Julia Kingsley was the stunner, not me!

Julia offered a hand and I wiped mine on my shorts before taking it. Hers was cool, her grip firm. Mine felt hot and damp by comparison.

She smiled, showing white, perfectly even teeth. Long gold earrings glinted in the hair that fell over her shoulders. "We're glad to have you here. We really are."

"I'm glad to be here," I said, and at that moment it was the absolute truth.

CHAPTER THREE

Phillip (I couldn't go on forever thinking of him only as Phillip Kingsley, and "Dad" seemed impossible, so I was preparing myself to call him by his first name) decided that Tad should come along on my tour of the theatre so we could "start getting to know each other." What I knew about Tad so far did not make me eager to know more. The kid had been on all through dinner, making wisecracks and jokes and doing his best to monopolize every conversation anybody got started. Everybody put up with him, but a couple of times I caught George rolling his eyes at another actor instead of laughing at one of Tad's jokes. The kid was rude and obnoxious. And totally spoiled. So far, he had managed to ignore me almost completely, and if he thought it would make me feel bad, he was wrong.

We had come into the theatre through the lobby doors, and when they had swung shut, they had cut off the light. Now I was standing on the steep slant of the right aisle as I waited for Phillip to turn on what he called the "houselights." I could hear voices and the thump of the actors' feet going up to the second-floor rehearsal hall, but I was in darkness so complete, it was like something solid against my face. There was a weird smell, too—of age, of dust maybe, and on top of that the sharp smell of new wood and fresh paint. Tad had gone on down the aisle in the dark, but I didn't feel like moving on the slanted floor, since I couldn't see so much as my hand in front of my nose.

Finally, two huge crystal chandeliers blinked on overhead and then a row of lights along the walls on either side. Tad was draped across the arm of an aisle seat near the stage, in an attitude of total boredom. A row of stage lights blazed on, lighting up heavy gold curtains with a deep red fringe across the front of the stage.

Phillip pushed through the curtains and came to the edge of the stage. "So—what do you think? They've done a great restoration job, haven't they?"

I nodded. The red carpet down the aisles, like the seats, was worn and faded. But the archway around the stage, all three-dimensional flowers and leaves and curlicue vines winding around each other, gleamed with fresh gold leaf. In the center, above the stage, two white plaster cherubs that looked like they were floating in front of the arch held between them a crest engraved with an elaborate golden *A*.

"Pretty," I said, moving down the aisle.

"This place was really something in its day. The pride of the town. Come up on the stage. I'll open the curtains. The steps are stage left."

I looked to the left and didn't see any steps. "What? Where?" I asked as Phillip disappeared again.

"*Stage* left, *stage* left," Tad said, pointing to the right. "Not *house* left!" He said it with the tone you might use with a slow two-year-old. I saw the four steps he was pointing to. "Stage left is left for the actor. House left is left for the audience. The steps are stage left—house right."

"Got it," I said. For a split second, I'd considered pretending that I knew all that and just hadn't heard what Phillip said, but no way I knew enough about theatre to compete with this kid. There was no point trying to hide it.

The curtains opened with a soft whir. Except for a dim bare-bulbed floor lamp set in the middle, the stage was empty. On either side were three narrow black velvet curtains. Across the back hung a flat piece of canvas with an elaborately painted scene—a forest with a mountain rising behind, its summit almost disappearing among rosy pink clouds.

"That's one of the original drops," Phillip said. "They found three of them still hanging up there in the stage house." He pointed up to the vast dark space above the stage. "One was damaged beyond repair, but they restored the others."

"Will you be using it for *Richard*?"

Tad laughed. "Oh, sure. We're doing *Richard* of the Rocky Mountains!"

"Tad, chill! We won't be using the drops for *Richard*, or the blacks behind them, either, for that matter. But it's great to have the original drops. It gives the place such a sense of history. Nothing much was changed when it was turned into a movie house—they just hung up a screen. The gas lights had been gone a long time by then, of course, but aside from that, this is as close to a genuine nineteenth-century theatre as you're likely to find anywhere. Beautiful, isn't it?"

I nodded again. "Beautiful!" I wasn't all that blown away, but it was what he expected me to say. I climbed the stairs up onto the stage and Tad got up and followed. I turned and looked out at the house, at the rows of red seats, trying to imagine myself up here, saying lines, with people in all those seats. It made me shiver even to think of it.

Tad came and stood next to me. He did a couple of tap-dance steps and took a bow to an imaginary audience. Then he turned to me. "Okay, here's how it goes. Stage left," he said, pointing to our left, "stage right." He turned and pointed at the drop. "Upstage." He turned back and pointed at the edge of the stage. "Downstage. The reason they used *up* and *down* is because stages used to be *raked*. That means they were slanted, high at the back, low at the front. Up and down."

"Thanks," I said.

"Anytime."

"What's the lamp for?" I asked Phillip. "I know that can't be for the *Richard* set."

Tad answered before Phillip could so much as open his mouth. "It's the ghost light. Haven't you even seen any old movies about the theatre?"

Phillip nodded. "It's just here to keep some light on the stage between rehearsals or performances. It's a safety thing—and a whole lot cheaper than leaving the work lights on!"

Ghosts again. "So, is it called a ghost light because it's supposed to keep away the ghosts?"

There was just the tiniest moment, just an eye-blink, before Tad scoffed. "Yeah, right! It keeps away the ghosts!"

Phillip went out through the side curtains and turned off the stage lights and the houselights. If somebody believed in ghosts, I thought, the ghost light wouldn't make them feel all that much better. It left a whole lot of very dark shadows. I followed Tad and Phillip into the hall leading to the dressing rooms. Phillip talked about the renovations as we went, and for a change, Tad didn't interrupt.

Upstairs, the rehearsal hall was a gigantic open room, its tall windows so dirty the late sunlight could hardly make its way through them. At one end of the room, the plain wooden floor was marked with tape in several colors, to show the edges of the stage and where the set would be. In the center was an old wooden army cot; otherwise, the stage was bare. The actors, in jeans or shorts and T-shirts, sat around the edges of the room on folding chairs. Some of them were smoking, dropping their ashes into Styrofoam coffee cups as they read over their scripts.

Laurence, the black guy Phillip had introduced as the fencing coach, was reading a magazine, and George was working a crossword puzzle. Toni sat behind a small table with a huge three-ring binder open in front of her. She drank from a bottle of springwater while she penciled notes on the pages. Tad pulled a folding chair up, sat next to her, and began teasing—turning pages, snatching at her pencil. She batted at him, like a cat with its claws pulled in, but just barely. She looked like she'd have preferred to smack him a good one.

Julia Kingsley wasn't there. She was playing Lady Anne, the woman Richard manages to persuade to marry him. Lady Anne wasn't in the scenes they were rehearsing tonight. I was disappointed about that, but otherwise I was sort of looking forward to the rehearsal, since I didn't have to do anything. It's pretty hard to understand Shakespeare just reading him—at least for me—but watching the movies had helped. And it's a great story. Richard, the Duke of Gloucester, wants to be king of England when the old king dies, but there are a bunch of other people in line for the crown before him. So he kills them. Or, like a Mafia godfather, has them killed—including his nephews, the two princes Tad and I were going to play. For a while, it looks like the bad guy's going to win—Richard gets the guys around him to do everything he wants them to do, mostly by promising them big rewards when he's in power, and manages to have himself crowned king. But some of his henchmen get scared off by the murders and turn against him, and when he doesn't live up to the promises he made, he loses some others. Finally, he gets killed in a battle to keep his crown. Sad end for Richard, happy end for everyone else, except all the people he's killed.

I had tried saying some of my character's lines out loud. But the language is so weird that I couldn't make it sound like a regular person talking, the way the actors in the movies could. I hoped these actors could do it, too, and I could learn how. If I didn't have any choice about acting, at least I didn't want to make a fool of myself doing it.

Phillip dumped Tad from the chair next to Toni's and straddled it himself. He motioned me to an empty chair and Tad to another. "Let me fill you in on the way we're playing *Richard* before we begin, Jared, so you can get a sense of it. We're not doing it with period sets and costumes. We're updating and changing it a little."

"You mean like the movie with Ian McKellen?"

"The kid's been doing his homework!" he said to

Tad. "Would that certain others would do so much." He turned back to me. "Yes and no. McKellen's version updated it to the thirties—a Nazi-like motif. We're going further. They say that the reason *Richard* has been so successful, from Shakespeare's time right down to today, is that it's universal. Timeless. Not so much English history as myth. So we're going to do a sort of *Star Wars* version."

"*Star Wars?*"

"Well, not literally. You remember how the original *Star Wars* movie starts?"

I nodded. I'd seen it so often, I practically had the whole trilogy memorized. "'Long ago,'" I started, and Tad, not to be outdone, joined in, "'in a galaxy far, far away...'"

"Right. The *Star Wars* movies combine myth—fairy tale really—with science fiction. That's what we're doing. Our setting will be a rocky planet where the people live mostly underground and where a kind of feudal system functions. Like in *Star Wars*, the costumes will be a combination of old fairy tale and far-out futuristic. The soldiers will be something like the stormtroopers and their weapons will be part laser gun, part light saber. No robots, though. Richard will dress in black, his henchmen in dark gray, but no Darth Vader imitations."

"Won't people think that's sort of weird?"

Phillip laughed and shook his head. "I hope not! I think people will understand it all better in a context they're familiar with."

"We hope more people will come to a *Star Wars* version," Toni said.

George looked up from his crossword. "A possibly vain hope, but it's worth a shot."

Phillip frowned at George. "Thank you, Mr. Sunshine. We all appreciate your optimism. All right! Places for scene four," he called. "The Tower." He stood up, turned, and sat properly in the chair. Then he turned back to Tad, who was trying to balance his chair on its back legs. "If you're going to stay, settle!"

Two actors went to the tape-marked stage and stood to one side, waiting for the signal to begin. One was Laurence; the other, the chunky redhead whose name, I thought, was Dennis. They looked like regular guys, Laurence in khakis and Nikes, Dennis in sandals, a Grateful Dead T-shirt, and cut-offs. But then, as they stood there in the silence, they seemed to change. I blinked. Laurence, playing the jailer, seemed almost to grow taller as he straightened his back and shoulders. Dennis, playing Richard's brother Clarence, took on a slump, his head jutting forward, his hands starting to work nervously at his sides.

"Lights up," Toni said, and the two moved forward onto the stage.

"Why looks your grace so heavily today?" Laurence said.

"O, I have passed a miserable night," Dennis answered, his hands clenching and unclenching, "so full of ugly sights, of ghastly dreams...."

When Toni called, "End of scene, end of act one," I would have applauded, except that nobody else did. Once the two murderers came into the scene, it had been funny! At one point, I'd laughed right out loud.

It had been a little like something out of a comic gangster movie. Richard had gotten the king to put his brother Clarence in prison, but now he wanted him killed. So he'd hired a couple of contract killers. George played the dumber one and Kent, who wore a nose ring and had tattoos on both his arms, the meaner one. When they got into his prison cell, Clarence started arguing with them and very nearly talked them out of it. The character George played was having trouble with his really warped conscience until the other reminded him of the money Richard had promised them. But even then, he kept dithering about it. He was still dithering when the meaner one finally just stabbed Clarence and dragged his body off to hide it.

As the actors, back to their normal selves now, settled in their chairs, Phillip turned to me. "Most directors cut that scene down to nothing, but I like it. Shakespeare knew what he was doing—*Star Wars* or traditional, this play needs all the comic relief it can get."

CHAPTER FOUR

By the time we got back from rehearsal, I could hardly keep my eyes open. It hardly seemed possible I'd left Cincinnati just that morning. It felt like I'd come to a completely different world—so far from everything I'd ever known that it ought to have taken about a week to get here. As soon as I'd answered everybody's questions about how I'd liked my first rehearsal and admired the sweater Joan was knitting for her grandson, I went up to Tad's and my room.

Tad, Hamlet trailing after him, started into the living room to watch some movie a couple of the actors had gotten at the video store, but Julia made him put Hamlet outside and sent him up after me with instructions to go straight to bed. I heard him kicking the backs of the steps as he came up, muttering about having had to waste a whole night at a rehearsal he wasn't even in, so I grabbed my toothbrush, my pajamas, and the towel and washcloth somebody had put out on my futon and got into the bathroom first. When I came back to the room, Tad was sitting cross-legged on his bed, making something out of Legos.

"Think you're so smart, don't you?" Tad said. "Talking about Ian McKellen's *Richard*."

I waded through the mess and hung my towel on a dresser-drawer knob. "I saw the one with Olivier, too," I said. "And Al Pacino's."

"Well, movies are a whole lot different from the stage, so don't think it's going to help you all that much. Have you ever acted in *anything* before?"

I shook my head.

"Huh!" Tad said, as if that proved something. "I'd been in two plays by the time I was four. And I've been in five movies—"

"And a soap opera," I finished for him. "I know."

I'd just gotten into bed when there was a knock at the door and Julia stuck her head in. "Sleep, Tad, not play." She waved at the mess on the floor. "But do something about all this before you go to bed. There's a laundry basket under there somewhere! At least get all your stuff on your side of the room. Jared has to have someplace to put his belongings. You okay?" she asked me. "Anything you need?"

"I'm fine," I said.

When she'd left, Tad shoved a few things away

from the door with one foot, then dug a couple of comic books out from under a heap of dirty underwear and headed for the bathroom, slamming the door behind him. He was gone so long, he might just as well have stayed downstairs and watched the movie. I'd been asleep long enough to have a dream about Serena getting a part in a big movie with Ian McKellen and telling Pop I could come live with her on location in a tent, when Tad came back. I pretended I was still asleep while he crashed drawers, opened and then slammed the closet door, and generally made enough noise to wake the dead. I didn't move so much as an eyelash.

In the morning, I woke up to go to the bathroom just after dawn. Tad was asleep, making little puffs of sound through his lips, like a horse. I decided I might as well just get dressed and get out of there, because I had a feeling that the less I saw of Tad when he was awake, the better chance I'd have getting along with him.

In the kitchen, I poured orange juice into a chipped Flintstones glass and went to sit on the concrete steps outside the back door. Hamlet, lying in his doghouse with his nose sticking out, opened his eyes. His tail made a slow *thump-thump*, but he didn't get up. It's even too early for dogs, I thought with a yawn. Way too early for me.

The sky still had that milky gray look it gets before the sun is high enough to make it blue. It was Pop's favorite time of day, *when nothing's certain yet and everything's possible.* I wondered how he was doing, whether he could move his left hand yet, and when he would think I'd settled in long enough that he could call me.

"Ack!" The voice and the screen door opening behind me startled me so that I practically levitated off the step. Orange juice splashed down my front.

"You scared me." Toni, dressed in an oversized T-shirt, came out onto the stoop. "There's never anybody up at this hour."

"You scared me, too," I said, swiping at the juice that was soaking into my shirt.

"Don't tell on me, okay?"

"Tell what?"

She waved an unlit cigarette at me. "I quit last week. George bet me I couldn't stay off 'em for a month." She cupped her hand over the end of the cigarette and flipped a plastic lighter to light it.

"You lose," I said.

"Not if he doesn't know. They're right about nicotine, you know. I am totally addicted! Don't ever start." She sat down next to me, stretching her legs out in front of her so that her bare feet touched the wet grass, and took a long, slow drag. "What're you doing up at this hour?"

I shrugged and lied. "I couldn't sleep."

"Me neither. I was dreaming of packs of dancing cigarettes, like those old-time TV commercials." She puffed for a moment, looking at the dog through half-closed eyes. "That dumb dog doesn't seem to have any trouble sleeping in. Except when Tad's around, he's the most laid-back canine I've ever seen. A dog of very little brain."

If he likes Tad, I thought, he has to be a dog of very little brain.

Toni blew smoke out of the side of her mouth and turned to look at me. "So. The Prince of Wales. You ever acted before?"

I shook my head.

"No sweat. Your dad's great. And I heard your mom acts, too."

She didn't give me time to answer. "So that means you've got acting genes from both sides. It's in the blood. Like Tad." Toni took a quick puff of her cigarette and went on. "Course, he started practically in the cradle. He's probably made more money than all the rest of us put together. Maybe even including Phillip and Julia."

I watched Hamlet's ear twitch as a fly landed on it. He didn't open his eyes.

"You gotta feel sorry for him, though. He's got the adolescent pudge-uglies big time. That's why the soap writers killed off his character in that skiing accident." Toni leaned back and blew smoke straight up. "I think we all owe the creation of the New World Shakespeare Company to the fact that nobody wants to do close-ups of Tad right now. Until he grows into the kind of good looks he's bound to get from Phillip and Julia, they can keep him here away from the cameras, give him some classical training, and keep him acting. They're starting a theatre dynasty—like the Barrymores. And now you're part of it, too!"

She turned and stared at me, squinting her eyes and nodding her head. I felt my ears getting hot again. "Either you got over the uglies way early or you're gonna skip 'em altogether. You're downright gorgeous, that's what you are. No, that's not right. What's the word I want?" She waved her cigarette, dropping ashes onto her bare legs. "Ethereal. That's it! Ethereal. Too bad we're not doing *A Midsummer Night's Dream*. You'd be perfect for Puck. Or Ariel in *The Tempest*. A sprite. All light and spirit. Unless there was some kind of genetic screwup and you can't act, you have a heck of a future in this business."

A teakettle started whistling in the kitchen, and Toni stubbed her cigarette out against the step and tossed the butt into the bushes. "Somebody's up. Probably Joan—fixing her ruddy English breakfast tea." She said that last with a British accent that made her sound exactly like the older woman. She pushed herself to her feet. "Guess I'll go in and put the coffee on. Come on in. She'll tell you some great stories. Ask her about the ghost of the Theatre Royal—before Tad gets up." At the door, Toni paused. "You're really lucky to be a part of this company, you know. I'd have killed to have had this kind of chance at your age."

I swallowed the last of my orange juice and tried

to get a glimpse of my reflection in the glass. "Ethereal," she had said. And Joan—she'd called me a "stunner." I had Serena's honey-colored hair, my cheekbones were too sharp and too high, and there was a cleft in my sort of pointed chin. That was from Phillip, I knew now—Tad had it, too. I'm not really skinny, but I'm not muscular, either. Serena says I've got a dancer's body. Just what you need to get along in Pop's and my downtown neighborhood! All my looks had ever done for me before was get me beat up. Even the girls in my school preferred the macho types who had to start shaving in the seventh grade. I guessed you had to be older to dig *ethereal*.

I got up and went over to Hamlet, who opened his eyes again and thumped his tail as I scratched behind his ears. "They ought to let you come inside," I told him. "Give you a decent bed." He just kept thumping, so I supposed he didn't mind. Maybe because he'd never lived any other way.

I went inside then and sat at the table, where Joan, in a puffy pink satin bathrobe, was pouring tea from a gold-trimmed teapot into a matching cup and saucer.

"He wants to hear about the Man in Gray," Toni said as she spooned coffee into the filter basket of a huge coffeepot.

"Ah!" Joan said, and her eyes crinkled up as she smiled. "I'll never forget the time I saw him. It was at the Theatre Royal, of course. He came during the final rehearsal of my Medea! He never comes to the shows, you know, only the rehearsals. But if he appears, you can be certain you have a hit on your hands." She took a sip of tea and smiled. "He was right, you know. The Medea notices were the best of my career!"

For the next half hour, as she sipped her tea and ate muffins with a yellow jam called lemon curd, Joan talked about the ghosts of the British theatre. To hear her tell it, practically every theatre in England had a ghost or two hanging around, helping actors or bringing luck, or playing tricks. Toni was right: The stories were good ones. The trouble was, Joan really seemed to believe them. Maybe after a lifetime of pretending to be other people all the time, you couldn't tell anymore what was made up and what was real.

When Joan went to her room to get dressed, Toni took me with her to pick up some doughnuts (smoking another cigarette in the van, driving with all the windows open to air out the smoke). Over the next couple of hours, the other members of the company straggled into the kitchen, looking barely awake. George was first, wearing a tattered plaid bathrobe, his long, skinny legs sticking out like stilts. He brought in the *New York Times* that had been left in a plastic bag on the front steps, then concocted something disgusting out of skim milk, several kinds of powder from white-labeled cans, a banana, and a carrot, whirled in the blender until it turned a sick yellowish brown. He drank it while reading the paper. As the others came down, poured coffee, and dug doughnuts out of the box, he clucked his tongue at them and muttered about fat and sugar and cholesterol. "Your arteries are closing up as we speak," he told Del, who took three. "You won't live to play Lear!" Del didn't answer. He just balanced his doughnuts on his coffee mug, picked up a section of the paper, and left, humming to himself.

Toni and George and Laurence were arguing about whether anybody would come to see *Richard*, whether the New World Shakespeare Company could make it in a town like Addison, and I was having my third glass of orange juice when Julia Kingsley came in. Looking at her took my breath away again, even though she wasn't wearing any makeup. She was dressed in bright blue loose-fitting pants and a man's shirt with its tails tied at the waist. She didn't greet anybody, just opened a cupboard door and pulled out a box of shredded wheat.

Toni and Laurence were agreeing with each other that Shakespeare would always get an audience because he was such a great playwright. Kent, who had taken his breakfast into the living room, off the kitchen, and was watching the *Today* show, hollered out that most Americans had never even seen a *play*, let alone one by Shakespeare.

"Exactly. Americans think of the Bard of Avon—those few who think of him at all—as homework," George said. "Like algebra, or grammar."

"That's why the *Star Wars* look," Laurence said.

"Oh, George, stop the doom and gloom," Julia said, getting a bowl for her cereal. "We'll make it. Aside from being a brilliant Lady Anne, I just happen to be the best fund-raiser east of the Mississippi and west of the Hudson. I got us three corporate sponsorships just this week!"

"That doesn't mean anybody'll actually come," George said, shaking the paper.

"They'll come," she said. "It'll be the class thing to do. Anybody who doesn't come'll look like an illiterate rube. It's a yuppie town; nobody wants to look like a rube." She sat down across the table from me and crumbled a shredded wheat biscuit into her bowl. "Did you sleep all right?" she asked me. I nodded. "Good. We've got some work for you and Tad to do today. It'll give you something to do besides hang around the rehearsal. Besides, doing a project together is a great way to get acquainted. There's a little dressing room that's been closed up—it's all full of junk. We're short of dressing room space, so we'd like the two of you to clear it out and clean it up. Once it's ready to use, it'll be yours."

Toni stood up, put her coffee cup in the sink, and rattled a huge set of keys. "Ten minutes to van departure!" she said. Then she stuck her head out into the hallway and bellowed it again, in a voice that could probably be heard all the way to the opera house. As she went past me, she opened her other hand to show me a cigarette, winked, banged open the screen door, and disappeared outside.

"Tad!" Julia called, as if he might not have heard. "Ten minutes! Come have some breakfast." She shook her head. "Just once I wish he'd get down here in time to eat a real breakfast."

Phillip strolled in, dropped a piece of wheat bread into the toaster, and picked up a section of the *Times*. "Anything interesting today?"

"Another Broadway drama closed," George said. "Great reviews, no audience."

"And a cheery good morning to you, too!"

"Look!" The voice from the hallway practically dripped with tragic horror. Everyone turned as Tad came in, tears streaming down both cheeks, holding up an airplane with shattered wings.

Tad pointed the plane at me like a missile launcher. *"Look what he did!"*

CHAPTER
FIVE

Tad's an actor, that's for sure. I was the only one
who wasn't taken in by his wailing. Julia looked
at Phillip in a "what do we do now" sort of way, and
Phillip just shrugged and made a point of looking at
his watch. Then Julia looked at me.

"I don't know anything about it," I said.

"Who else could have done it?" Tad asked, gulp-
ing and choking on his tears.

Then I had an idea. Tad had to have broken his
own plane to get me in trouble. Maybe I could make
his little trick backfire on him. "I suppose I could
have stepped on it on my way out this morning.
There's a lot of stuff under all those clothes on the
floor."

Julia asked if he'd cleaned up the room yet, and
he shook his head, the tears still streaming down his

cheeks. "Well then, no wonder something got broken," she said. "Jared can't move in there without stepping on something of yours. Before dinner tonight, I want everything up off the floor." Then she looked from me to Tad and back to me again and sighed. "It's too bad you can't have rooms of your own, but I'm sure you can work out a way to share the space."

"Of course they can," Phillip said. "Now let's get this show on the road." The look Tad gave me as I followed Toni out to the van could have curdled milk.

Before rehearsal started that morning, Toni handed me a bucket full of cleaning supplies and a big old push broom. "You kids are supposed to clean out the little dressing room today."

I nodded, but I must not have looked any more enthusiastic than I felt, because she winked. "Listen, it's better than cleaning the johns, and somebody's got to do that, too! We don't have any apprentices in the company to do the scut work. Besides, in return, you guys get to have your own dressing room. Like stars!" She looked around the rehearsal room. "I don't know where Tad's gotten to, but I'm sure he'll be along in a minute. You go ahead and get started. I'll send him down as soon as he shows up."

As I headed down the stairs, I thought it might be better to work by myself anyway. After the trick Tad had pulled with the airplane, I wasn't exactly looking forward to spending the morning with him.

41

I hoped whatever the room needed, it wasn't going to be much real work. By the time I got to the bottom of the steps, I was already starting to sweat. The air-conditioning vents were kept closed everywhere in the building except where people were actually rehearsing (to save money) and this part of the theatre was uncomfortably warm.

I heard a voice down the hallway. The sound came from the larger of the two men's dressing rooms. Bright light spilled from the open door. As I got closer, I could tell it was someone going over lines. "Excuse me," I called, and the voice stopped. "Could you tell me where the little dressing room is? The one I'm supposed to clean?"

It was George, who stuck his head out into the hall, his script in his hand, his eyebrows knitted. "I can tell you where it is"—he looked down the hall, first one way and then another, as if checking to see whether someone was listening, then lowered his voice to an ominous stage whisper—"but I wouldn't go in there if I were you."

"Why not?"

"Never mind why not. Nobody believes me anyway." George pointed with his script down the hallway toward the stage. "It's the door opposite the first set of legs."

"Legs?"

"Side curtains. That room was closed up when the company moved in here, and if you ask me, they should just leave it that way. Of course, nobody asks me." With that, George disappeared.

The stage was even darker than the hall, with only the ghost light lit. The three heavy black velvet side curtains were like sentinels guarding it. I could see why they called them "legs"—each was half of a pair, one stage left, the other stage right. I found the dressing room door, turned the knob, and pulled. With a creaking and groaning of corroded hinges, the door opened. Inside, the room was pitch-black. What little light spilled around the curtains from the stage lamp didn't do anything for the dressing room. I felt for a light switch on the wall and found it. Not a regular light switch—it had to be pushed in instead of flipped up. Odd, I thought, as a bulb hanging down from the ceiling on a frayed cord flicked on. The wiring everywhere else in the building had been brought up-to-date, but the electricians must have forgotten this room. The bulb, big and old-fashioned-looking, couldn't have been more than a forty-watter. The dim light it threw onto stacks of boxes, broken chairs, and a clothes rack full of dusty, drooping clothes made heavy shadows, accentuating the darkness more than the light. And the brown painted walls didn't help. The spray cleaner and rags in my bucket wouldn't change those. What this room needed was about a gallon of white paint.

On the wall to my right, above a dusty counter stacked with junk—broken stage lights, coils of rope, and open cartons full of unidentifiable bits and pieces of stage hardware—were two round mirrors, their silver streaked and pitted. On either side of each was a porcelain light fixture with a turn knob at the base. Each fixture held a single bulb that looked no better than the one overhead. Still, five of them had to be better than one. I went in to turn them on.

The door banged shut behind me, startling me so that I yelped.

I froze, expecting to hear laughter, or the sound of footsteps heading back down the hall. I figured it was George who had slammed the door, setting me up with all that stuff about keeping the room closed up so he could play a trick on me. Toni had said he liked messing with people's heads. But through the closed door, I could still hear the muffled sound of his voice from the dressing room down the hall. Maybe the door was hung off balance on its hinges, somehow, I thought. Maybe it just wouldn't stay open by itself.

I turned the switches on each of the four mirror lights. Only one of the bulbs came on. As I'd expected, it was no brighter than the bulb overhead. Still, I was grateful for what little light it added. I made a mental note to ask Toni where to get new bulbs—hundred-watters at least.

I shivered. The room, now that the door was closed, was almost chilly. Dank. Instead of the smell of fresh paint and new wood that was nearly everywhere else in the building, here all I could smell was old dust and mildew. And something else I couldn't identify—something nasty. It made my nose tingle and I sneezed. No wonder George wouldn't come in.

Maybe the room had been forgotten during the

renovations, I thought, or maybe the workmen came in, took one breath, and decided this little bit of space—not much more than a big closet—wasn't worth fixing. I opened the door, which creaked and groaned again, and propped it with one of the broken chairs.

I looked around, thinking it might be better to have to clean the johns. What was I supposed to do with all the junk? There was no way to clean without getting it out of the way first. The room had been used like a Dumpster for a long, long time. There probably wasn't anything in it worth saving. But I couldn't very well be the one to decide what to keep and what to throw away. I dropped the bucket and broom on the floor and sighed. The only thing I could do was just put stuff out in the hall and let somebody else deal with it.

I took a breath through my mouth instead of my nose. Better. When I went looking for some brighter lightbulbs, I would see if I could get some kind of room deodorizer, too.

I started to work, pulling boxes out into the hall, stacking them against the wall next to the door. When I'd cleared the boxes out from in front of the clothes rack, I saw that it had wheels, so I pushed it out into the hall and down to the brightly lit white-painted dressing room where George was sitting in front of an electric fan, his feet up on the counter, speaking his lines into the mirror. He stopped and looked over at me. "Well?"

"These look like old costumes. Do you know what I should do with them?"

George glanced at the rack and shook his head. "No good for this show. But Phyllis, the costumer, might get a kick out of going through them. Looks like they could have been here most of this century." He wrinkled his nose. "Smells like it, too. Just leave the rack in the hall, unless you want to take it to the costume shop."

I didn't know where the costume shop was, so I left the rack there in the hall.

When I got back to the little dressing room, both of the lights were off. I hadn't turned them off when I left. Old as they were, the bulbs must have burned out, I decided. I'd have to find more bulbs before I could go on with the job. Just to be sure, I tried the switch on the wall inside the door. The overhead bulb came on. I stood for a moment, trying to sort it out. Somebody *had* turned the lights off. But who? Tad, playing tricks on me? Where was he, anyway?

I stood in the doorway for a moment, not really wanting to go in and try the other light. But then I got hold of myself. It was only an empty room. Gloomy and smelly and depressing, but only a room. I went to the mirror and reached for the switch. And caught a glimpse of movement behind me. I spun around. There was no one there. My heart was beating so fast, I put my hand on my chest as if I could hold it down. Dumb. Totally dumb. I gave myself a sort of mental shake and then, very slowly and deliberately, I turned back and twisted the switch on the mirror light.

The bulb flicked on. And in the mirror I saw what might have been a face, dim and unfocused, hovering slightly above my left shoulder. I felt the hairs on the back of my neck fizz. I blinked. But the shape remained where it had been, smudgy and undefined. Just that. Just a shape like a face, with dark spaces that could be eyes, a line of nose, a shadow of mouth.

I felt a chill in the pit of my stomach. "Dumb," I whispered out loud. "It's nothing but an old smudgy mirror. There's nothing there."

Before I could turn around again, the two light-bulbs, both at the same moment, flared blue and burned out, leaving a scent of hot dust in the darkness.

CHAPTER
SIX

It was only the run up the stairs that made my heart beat so hard, I thought as I got to the rehearsal hall. Only the run up the stairs.

The rehearsal was going on, and I dared not interrupt Toni to ask about lightbulbs, so I leaned against the wall and waited till my heart slowed down and I could breathe again. I wasn't about to go back to the dressing room without lightbulbs. I didn't want to go back at all, actually. Too dark, too smelly, and probably dangerous because of the old wiring. I refused to so much as think about what I'd thought I'd seen in the mirror.

Once my breath was coming a little more evenly, I sat down in an empty chair at the back of the room. I'd already gotten caught up in the rehearsal. Phillip wasn't just directing; he was also playing Richard.

Watching him move around the tape-marked stage, I could hardly believe the difference between what I knew of Phillip Kingsley the man and the character he was playing. There was the physical difference— a slight limp, a tiny change in posture, a different tone in the voice. But the effect was a lot more than that. A cartoonist came to school one time and did a demonstration that showed how much difference the slant of a single line—an eyebrow, or a mouth— could make in a cartoon character's expression. This was like that.

In the scene they were doing, Richard's secret allies were publicly begging him to take the crown, while he refused it, pretending that the last thing he wanted in the whole world was to be king. When I had first read the scene, I thought Richard's trick seemed too obvious, that no one with half a brain could have been fooled by it. But Phillip made the trick work. I could see that all Richard had to be to pull it off was a good actor.

Phillip wasn't playing the part as a movie kind of villain—a Darth Vader type. As he refused the crown, Phillip's Richard came across not as evil but as...sad maybe. And hurt—wounded. Even though I knew it was only a trick, I could almost believe him when he said being king would be too much for him.

But it wasn't only the sad, wounded Richard that came across. There was something dark underneath, like a shadow. It was that shadow that was the most amazing. Even in rehearsal, wearing regular clothes,

Phillip Kingsley could become this whole other person *and* he could make an audience believe two different things about him at the same time. I wondered, if I turned out to be able to act at all, if I could ever hope to be as good as that.

When the break was announced, before I had a chance to get to Toni, Julia came over. "Done so soon?" she asked. "Where's Tad?"

"I don't know," I said. "I haven't seen him."

"Toni?" Julia called. "Didn't you send Tad down to work on the little dressing room with Jared?"

Toni stood up from her place and stretched. "I never got a chance. He didn't come up before we started."

Julia sighed. "He's probably down in the costume shop. You didn't get that dressing room all cleaned out by yourself in this much time...."

I shook my head. "The lightbulbs burned out—both of them—so I couldn't do any more. I came up to ask Toni for some bulbs. Big ones."

"I'm sure we have some one hundreds. Tad knows where they're kept. I'll have him bring them down. Toni, when you get a minute, find Jared a flashlight, would you?"

Ten minutes later, walking with a kind of resentful swagger, Tad showed up outside the dressing room with a package of lightbulbs. From the look on his face, I figured Julia had chewed him out.

I held up the flashlight. "You want to hold the flashlight or change the bulbs? It doesn't matter to me."

"It doesn't matter to me, either." For a moment, we just stood there, staring at each other. He was chewing gum, and the hair around his face was stuck to his skin again with sweat. A zit was starting on his chin, red and angry-looking. Toni wasn't kidding about the adolescent uglies, I thought. "I'll do the bulbs," he said.

The dressing room door was still propped open with the broken chair. I turned the flashlight on and went in, shining it on the fixture next to the first mirror. It would take a ladder to change the overhead bulb.

"Peee-yoouuu," Tad said as he started into the room. "It stinks. What'd you do, let one in here?"

I didn't say anything. The light from the flashlight, which had seemed strong enough when I turned it on, had faded. Its beam, gold now, barely pushed back the darkness in the room. Tad stood still, just inside the doorway. The dankness and smell of the room seemed even worse than before. Still Tad didn't move. "Well?" I said. I moved the flashlight beam from one light to the other. "There they are."

"You weren't supposed to open the air-conditioning vents."

"There aren't any vents in here." I played the flashlight beam around the room to show him. Still Tad didn't move.

"I'll do it if you're afraid of the dark," I said as Tad backed up a step and leaned against the doorway.

"I'm not afraid of anything."

I went over to get the bulbs. Suddenly, without planning it, I found myself leaning close to him and whispering in the same sort of ominous whisper George had used, "Not even the *ghost*?"

There was the tiniest pause. "Ghost?" His voice squeaked.

I kept my voice light. "Sure. You know, the one that scared George so bad, he won't come in here. The one that scared the renovators away from this room. Why do you think it used to be kept closed up?" I set the flashlight on the counter and started to unscrew the first bulb. "I thought I saw him before—the ghost. In the mirror there."

"You can't scare me."

I already did, I thought, and stifled a grin. I could see it in his eyes. Served him right for trying to leave this whole job to me. I screwed in a new bulb, blinking in the sudden brightness as it came on. Quickly, not looking into either mirror as I worked, I unscrewed the other bulbs, dropped them into a box of junk, and put new ones in each socket. I switched the lights on, and for the first time, the room was really light. It was still dingy and gloomy, as if the brown of its walls sucked light in somehow. But it wasn't dark.

I looked at the mirrors, finally. No face there except my own, blurry and vaguely distorted. Of course not. The image I'd seen before—I *thought* I'd seen—had just been a trick of the dim light, the distortion of the old mirrors.

Tad, popping his gum, came all the way in, his shoulders back, as if to prove he hadn't been scared. "So let's get started. The sooner we start, the sooner we'll get out of here."

"Okay. You drag boxes out in the hall." Without waiting for a response, I started sweeping in the corner where the clothes rack had been.

When the rest of the boxes were out in the hall and the floor swept, I took the glass cleaner and a roll of paper towels out of the bucket and set them on the counter in front of Tad. "I'm going to get some water to wash the counter. You do the mirrors."

"What if I don't want to?" Tad spit his gum into his hand, stuck it to the underside of the counter, then reached into his pocket and took out a slightly bent cigarette and a pack of matches. Leaning against the counter, he struck a match and nonchalantly lit the cigarette and took a drag.

I just stood there, staring. This was the kid with a whole roomful of toys. "Where'd you get that?"

He took another drag, coughed a little, and flipped an ash on the floor I'd just swept. "None of your business."

"Phillip and Julia know you smoke?" I asked him.

"Who says I do? You tell 'em and I'll deny it."

I shrugged. "Why would I bother telling? It's your funeral." I picked up the bucket. "I'm going to get the water. The mirrors are your job."

"You're not the boss of me."

I felt something inside me slip. Maybe it was having to work in this awful little room, or maybe it was just Tad. "Listen here, you little creep." I dropped the bucket back on the counter. "I'm sorry if you don't want a brother. I wasn't exactly looking for one, either. But it's not my fault. So there's no point taking it out on me."

Tad blew smoke at me. "I'm my father's only *legal* son."

I blinked against the smoke, fighting the urge to knock the cigarette out of his hand. "Yeah? Well, I'm his *firstborn*."

"So your mother says." He stubbed the cigarette out against the countertop and dropped it into the bucket. "Maybe she was just some summer-stock apprentice who messed around with every actor in the company and picked my father to blame when she got knocked up."

I felt my fists clench, but before I could say or do anything, one of the lightbulbs flared and blew out. Tad yelped. Just then, I saw that dim shape in the mirror again, like a face hovering in the air behind me. Was it smiling? The hairs on the back of my neck fizzed again.

With a blue flash, another bulb blew out. I went out into the hall and kicked away the chair that held the door propped open. The door slammed shut. A moment later, Tad screamed.

CHAPTER SEVEN

Tad was so hysterical, by the time everybody got down from rehearsal to see what he was screaming about, that he threw up all over the hall. No acting this time. Between sobs and barfing, he managed to get out just enough actual words to let everybody know that there was a ghost in the little dressing room. He'd seen him in the mirror.

"I asked you not to say anything," Julia said, glowering at George as she mopped Tad's face with a wet washcloth Toni had brought. "I was afraid this would happen...."

George shook his head. "I never said a word. He saw what he saw—"

Julia stopped him with a look and took Tad off to get him cleaned up.

"I'm telling you, that dressing room's a nasty

place," George said to Phillip when they'd gone. "If I were you, I'd close it up again and leave it closed. Padlock it!"

"Don't be ridiculous," Phillip said. "We need the space. Tad has a good imagination, and he was startled by the lights going out, that's all. We'll get the wiring fixed and it'll be fine." He shook his head. "Then, if some people would keep their big mouths shut—"

"It isn't my mouth you need to worry about," George said. "It's the ghost. It's real."

"Enough! Everybody back to rehearsal." Phillip shooed the others down the hallway and then turned back to George. "I don't want to hear that word again!"

George shrugged and went into the big dressing room as the others headed back upstairs, arguing as they went. I could hear Joan's voice above the others. "I tell you, I saw the Man in Gray at the Theatre Royal with my own eyes!"

When they had gone, I didn't know what to do. I had no intention of cleaning up the disgusting mess Tad had made. And I wasn't going to go back into the dressing room. I didn't believe in George's ghost. Or any of Joan's, either. But Tad wasn't the only one with a good imagination. That facelike smudge in the mirror only showed from a certain angle, but it gave me the creeps. I didn't want to see it again.

Since nobody had given me a job, I supposed I

could do anything I wanted. I decided to explore the building. There was a lot more to it than I'd seen so far. I propped the dressing room door with the chair again and went in just long enough to grab the flashlight.

An hour later, I'd been into every nook and cranny of the old building. It was honeycombed with narrow halls and passageways designed to get actors from dressing rooms to backstage, from one side of backstage to the other, even up to the attic, where there were openings in the theatre ceiling for stage lights and the cables that connected them to the electrical system.

When I'd finished my exploration, I ended up in the basement, in a big dirt-floored space under the stage, another place the renovators hadn't gotten to. It, too, had only a dim bulb for light just inside the door. The place was draped with cobwebs and full of dust that had made me sneeze the moment I shoved the sliding door out of the way and ventured in. The flashlight beam had showed me the reason the peeling sign next to the door read TRAP ROOM. Its ceiling, which was the underside of the stage floor, was full of trapdoors, hinged and latched shut.

The traps had to be the way what Serena called "theatre magic" could happen. Like ghosts. You could open a trap, send a puff of smoke up through the hole, then send up an actor in a filmy costume. To the audience, it would look like a ghost materializing out of the smoke—and it could disappear again just as fast.

I was sitting on an old box now, and I sneezed again. The dust and dirt were getting to me, but I hated to leave. Grubby as it was, I liked this place. Maybe nobody even remembered it was here. Maybe no one had been in here since the opera house had been a real theatre. It would make a great hideout. A place I could have all to myself, that I wouldn't have to share with Tad.

Ghosts. There were ghosts in the play. A whole bunch of them had to appear to Richard right near the end. My heart sank. What if Phillip was planning to use the traps for that scene? No way I could have a hideout if people were going to be coming in and out all the time. I shone the flashlight around the whole space. Here, like in the little dressing room, people had stored junk—boxes, old props and set pieces, scenery flats.

I could still make myself a hiding place down here, I realized. I could use the junk stored here to create it. The room was plenty big enough. All I had to do was make a kind of junk barricade. I could wall off a space against the far wall without anything getting in the way of the traps. Nobody would ever have to know anything about it. How often would they be down here anyway?

There was a big old overstuffed chair in one corner with some boxes on it, and I'd seen a couple of rolled-up rugs in the other room in the basement where old props were stored. A chair and a rug and my tape player, some tapes and a few books, and I could be really comfortable. I couldn't help sharing a bedroom with Tad, a dressing room with Tad. But this place—a totally secret place—would be all mine!

I sat for a moment, looking up at the traps. The theatres in England that Joan had talked about probably had traps. And actors had a lot of time to fill when they weren't onstage or rehearsing. Maybe some of them used that time to play tricks on the others. The ghost stories Joan told could have started that way. A few tricks, some people like George and Joan who were easy to convince, and pretty soon you could have a whole theatre company believing in ghosts.

I decided to check out how the trapdoors worked. I moved the box I'd been sitting on underneath one, stood on the box, and unlatched the trap. Light from above made a line of light all around the edges as it opened. Cautiously, I poked my head up through the hole. The stage was deserted, lit only by that single standing lamp.

Ghost light, I thought. Wouldn't it be funny if a ghost—like one of Joan's tricksters—stole the ghost light? I boosted myself up through and unplugged the lamp. As I stood there in the sudden darkness, waiting for my eyes to adjust, I thought I felt a kind of chill against my skin. Like a draft. My stomach clenched and I clutched the lamp plug tighter, wires pricking my palm. Dumb. The backstage was hot and stuffy as well as dark. Imagination again. The pale square in the floor where the light from the flashlight glowed feebly from below was suddenly very inviting. I lowered the lamp through the trap, lowered myself after it, and then latched the trap-door back into place.

I set the lamp next to the Trap Room's sliding door. When I was sure the coast was clear, I'd take it out to the lobby and leave it with its cord wrapped neatly around its base. Pretty soon, Joan would have another story to add to her collection—a story about the trick-playing ghost of the Addison Opera House.

CHAPTER EIGHT

Toni noticed the lamp was missing before we left the theatre to go home for dinner that evening. She accused George of trying to scare everybody by leaving the stage in the pitch-dark. He denied it, of course.

Then, as everyone who was supposed to ride in the van was on the way out through the lobby, there it was, exactly where I'd put it, the cord wrapped around its base. "Who put this here?" Toni asked. No one answered. She gave George a disgusted look. "Some clown. Well, you can all just wait till I've taken it back where it belongs. It won't be my fault if we're late for dinner."

In a few minutes, she was back, still carrying the lamp, waving the plug in the air. "Look at this!" She showed us a halo of frayed wire around the plug.

"And look here! The cord is already scorched. Partly melted. This lamp was a disaster waiting to happen. We could have had a fire for sure. Think what could have happened if it had started on the stage while we were all upstairs rehearsing! We could all have been killed." But still nobody claimed to have moved the lamp.

"It was probably Phillip," Laurence said.

At dinner, of course, Phillip said he hadn't. And so did everyone else, except Tad, who wasn't there. He'd been too sick to his stomach to eat and he'd taken a bowl of chicken broth up to our room. Nobody thought to ask me, so I didn't have to lie.

"Could it have been one of the techies?" Toni asked.

"They're all still over at the college working on the set," Kent reminded her.

"So then—maybe it was the ghost," she said, almost but not quite joking.

I stopped chewing the bite of hamburger casserole I'd just taken.

"It's just the sort of thing the Man in Gray would do," Joan said. "He's watched over the Theatre Royal for more than a hundred years."

"Of course!" Toni crowed. "The ghost protecting his theatre! How absolutely terrific!"

I grinned. It was working! The ghost they were inventing wasn't the practical joker I'd meant him to be, but—just like a character in a play—he was beginning to seem real. To some people anyway.

George frowned into his cup of herbal tea. "If

I remember right, there are a whole slew of ghosts in the Theatre Royal, and not all of them are as friendly as the Man in Gray."

Julia shook her head. "This is ridiculous!"

"I'd rather be able to lay the whole thing to rest," Phillip Kingsley said, "but I suppose that's too much to ask. Let's just agree for now that if there *is* anything—otherworldly—in the building, it's a nice theatre-friendly guardian spirit."

Julia frowned at Phillip and George shook his head and said, "All I can say is that if there *is* a nice friendly ghost unplugging lamps in the Addison to save us all from a fire, it's not the one who hangs around the little dressing room. There's nothing the least bit friendly about that one!"

"Just what we need," Julia said. "More than one." I looked up from my plate and found her looking at me. "Don't forget there are a couple of impressionable young minds here."

"That's okay," I said. "I don't believe in ghosts."

"Well, Shakespeare did," George said. "And so do I." Joan nodded. So did Sam and Dennis. Kent, who not only had tattoos and a nose ring, but rode a motorcycle to the theatre, shook his head.

"Well, unless somebody's lying, it has to be a ghost. Who else could have moved that lamp?" Toni asked no one in particular.

The next morning, Laurence asked if I'd like a fencing lesson during rehearsal. Stage combat class was that evening, and he thought I might like a little preparation for it, since I'd never fenced before. "Tad's getting pretty good," he said. "If you can get a little extra practice in, the two of you could be fencing partners. He'll have an edge for a while, but if you work at it, you'll catch up fast. It'll be good for both of you."

Tad was getting good? I didn't like the idea of facing Tad with a sword in his hand—not even if I had one, too. "But I'm not going to be in any of the fight scenes," I said.

"It's not just for the show," Laurence said. "It's for grace and posture and stage presence. Every actor needs to take fencing."

"I'm a brown belt in karate. Won't that do?"

Laurence shrugged. "Couldn't hurt. It shows that you've got speed and strength and balance—but it isn't the same. You'll like fencing—you'll see. Look at me. Fencing isn't exactly the top African-American sport, but I wouldn't trade it for anything. I learned more than diction and acting in college. I learned"—he lowered his voice and winked—"that guys look great in fencing jackets. Much better than those pajama things they wear in karate. No woman can resist a fencer!"

"So where's your girlfriend?" I said.

He laughed. "Which one? I have to beat the women away with my foil!"

So, when I had hoped to be fixing up my hiding place in the Trap Room, I found myself moving furniture out of the way in the Greenroom (which isn't green at all, just what theatre people call the actors' lounge) so Laurence could give me my first fencing lesson. It wasn't a sword Tad would be swinging at me; it was a foil—long and skinny and bendy, with a round metal hand guard and a plastic tip on the sharp end, "so it's a sport," Laurence explained. "Without the tip and the mask and the padded jacket, the whole endeavor could be deadly. It used to be, back when men fought duels for their honor— or their lady's favor."

By the time my lesson was done, my legs were killing me. You have to keep your knees bent all the time and support your weight mostly with your thigh muscles. I had learned the proper way to stand—sideways to your opponent, but with your sword arm, your right leg, and your face turned toward him and your other arm held up and curved behind your head. I had also learned to lunge and thrust and parry, how to advance and retreat, and how important keeping a straight back and a loose wrist are. Laurence let me hit him a couple of times (it's called a hit or a "touch" when you get your opponent with the tip of your foil), and he went at me slowly enough that I could parry his thrusts sometimes, but if we'd been fighting for real, I would have died about a hundred times in my first match.

When he took off his mask, Laurence was grinning. "You're even quicker than I expected," he said.

"You're going to be giving Tad a run for his money in no time. Come to class tonight and I'll have Kent work with you. You wouldn't think it to look at him, but he's darned good! The best in the company except for Phillip—and me, of course."

So it wasn't till after lunch that I had a chance to get down to the Trap Room. I moved everything away from the far wall, making a space about eight feet long and almost that wide. In the prop storage area, I found a red Oriental rug that would just about match the big old red chair, and the perfect size. I lugged it and a pedestal table into the Trap Room, unrolled the rug to cover the dirt floor, dragged the chair onto it, and set the table next to the chair. The chair was dusty and moth-eaten, and in several places it leaked stuffing, but it was decently comfortable and very big. I brushed as much dust from it as I could, sneezing as I worked. Back in props, I found a scruffy brocade hassock and the perfect way to light my space—an old glass oil lamp. It was dirty and the chimney was cracked, but the base was about halfway full of oil.

Then I built the barricade that would keep my lair hidden even if someone came in. I used the scenery flats, lying on their sides, like walls, propping them against each other and leaving a narrow space against the left-hand wall of the room for an entrance. I used boxes and wooden chairs and other junk to hold them in place and to hide them at the same time.

When I was done, I went out and came back in to see whether anyone would be able to tell there was an empty space behind all the junk. Not likely. Not even if I was there, as long as I heard them coming in time to put my lamp out before they opened the door. All the traps were still accessible, so there would be no reason for anybody to have to move anything.

Except for the dust and cobwebs, my hideout was perfect. But I was a mess. I brushed as much dirt off my shirt and shorts as I could and headed up to the bathroom. I needed to wash up before I went up to the rehearsal hall to bum matches from somebody. I wanted to try out the oil lamp.

When I got to the first floor, the door to the little dressing room was propped open. Light poured out into the hall and I could hear men's voices arguing inside. The electricians were already there, working on the wiring. "Watch what you're doing, you idiot!" a deep voice roared. "You nearly took my finger off!"

"Well, keep it out of my way, then."

They sounded about as happy working together in that room as Tad and I had been. I cleaned up a little and went upstairs. There was a REHEARSAL IN PROGRESS sign on the doorknob. I let myself in as quietly as I could. They were working on a big scene, so most of the company was onstage. Tad, I saw, wasn't there.

Toni had heard me come in. She turned and,

holding her place in the script with a finger, beckoned me over. "Take this down to Phyllis in the costume shop," she whispered, handing me a sheet of measurements. "Then come back. I've got another errand for you to run." So much for trying out the oil lamp.

The costume shop was in a storefront building adjoining the theatre. A door connected them just behind the box office in the theatre lobby. When I got down there, the door was open, and I could see Hamlet inside, lying on the floor, with Tad next to him, playing with a radio-controlled Jeep. He'd been so frightened by the ghost the night before that he'd insisted on having Hamlet sleep on his bed instead of in the doghouse, and he had absolutely refused to come to the theatre without the dog, in spite of Phillip's objections. I went in and handed the page of measurements to Phyllis, who was working at one of the three sewing machines. Hamlet looked up and wagged his tail, but Tad ignored me and I ignored him.

"Thanks," Phyllis said. "Tell Toni I still need measurements on all the local actors."

"Okay," I said, and moved my foot just in time to keep Tad's Jeep from hitting me. I noticed a box of Legos under the ironing board and a toy chest in the corner. No wonder he hung out in the costume shop. It occurred to me that life for a kid in the theatre, unless you had a really big part, had to be awfully boring most of the time.

I went back up to the rehearsal hall then, and Toni gave me a list of drinks to get at the coffee-house on the other side of the town square, along with the cash to get them. "Try to get back before the coffee's cold and the yogaccinos are melted," she whispered. I nodded.

As I was leaving the coffeehouse a little while later with a handful of matchbooks in my pocket and box full of plastic-domed drinks, I saw Phyllis and Tad, with Hamlet on a leash, heading into the town square. Hamlet was stopping to lift his leg against every tree trunk. I ducked back inside and waited till they'd disappeared out of sight behind a bandstand ringed with bushes. Then I hurried back to the theatre as fast as I could go. I'd had an idea. The ghost of the Addison Opera House was about to show his trick-playing side.

I went into the costume shop and grabbed Tad's Jeep, leaving its remote control on the floor. Then, on an impulse, I snatched the spools from the sewing machines, pulling the thread free, and dropped them into the tall trash can at the end of the cutting table. The iron sat, unplugged, on the ironing board. I plugged it into the extension cord that snaked across the floor next to the Legos, turned the dial on high, and went out, closing the door behind me.

The little dressing room was still open and the lights were on, but I didn't hear the electricians inside. I peeked in. On either side of the mirrors and above them now were strips with four lightbulbs in each. Plenty of light. But the damp and smell hadn't gone away. The room wasn't much better with light than without it. I set the Jeep on the counter in front of the mirror farthest from the door and hurried back up to the rehearsal hall with the box of drinks. The actors were on break and swarmed around to get them.

"Stick around," Toni told me when she'd finished giving people their change, "in case somebody needs something else."

Rehearsal had just started again when Tad appeared with Hamlet still on his leash. He came straight to where I was sitting. "What did you do with my Jeep?" he whispered.

I turned to him with my best innocent look. "Jeep?"

"I know you took it. Where is it?"

I pretended to be too interested in the scene onstage to listen. I just shrugged and waved him away.

"Where is it?" Tad asked again, his voice louder.

Phillip, who was sitting on the edge of the stage manager's table, turned around and gave us a ferocious look.

I shrugged again.

"I asked what you did with my Jeep," Tad said in full voice. The actors stopped and looked our way.

"That's enough!" Phillip said. "If you can't be quiet, you may not be in here during rehearsal. You know better than that, Tad. Now go. Both of you! And take the dog with you!"

"But he—" Tad started.

"Go!" Phillip thundered. "Now!"

On the stairs, following Tad and Hamlet, I said, "If you mean that toy you were playing with before, I think I might have seen it in the dressing room as I came by. *Our* dressing room."

"'Might have seen it.' Oh, sure!"

When we were nearly to the dressing room, I saw that the light was off. Strange, I thought. It had been on a couple of minutes ago. Then, a few feet from the doorway, Hamlet stopped. Tad tugged at the leash, but the dog refused to move. He started to growl and the hair rose along the back of his neck and at the base of his tail. "Come on, Hamlet!" Tad said. "Let's go." The dog went on growling, his feet set wide apart, unmoving. Tad pulled and pulled at the leash, but Hamlet wouldn't move. Tad put on his most ferocious voice. "I said come! Come, Hamlet! What is the matter with you?"

Still Hamlet didn't move. His growl got deeper and louder.

"Never mind," Tad said finally, his voice shaky. "I don't need the stupid Jeep." He turned around and went back past me, Hamlet trotting beside him as if nothing had happened. And I was left by myself, goose bumps rising along both of my arms as I stared into the dark opening of the empty dressing room.

CHAPTER
NINE

I stood there for a long time, thinking about what George had said about that room. Thinking about lights going out and shapes in the mirror and damp and chill and smell. And the stuff I'd heard about animals hearing and seeing things—ghostly things—people couldn't. Then I rubbed away my goose bumps, swallowed a couple of times to get my saliva working again, and shoved those thoughts out of my mind. Toni had said it: Hamlet was a dog of very little brain. There was no need to worry about what he'd just done. Maybe he didn't like the smell. That's all it was, I told myself.

I went down to the Trap Room, glad to have someplace of my own to go to. Using the coffee-house matches, I lit the oil lamp. I had a little trouble at first adjusting the wick so the flame wouldn't smoke up the chimney, but when I got it turned down just enough, it threw a warm golden light. My hiding place, dark and shadowy before, had become a snug, cozy little room. I settled into the big comfortable chair with my *Richard* script. I'd watched enough rehearsals now to know that the sooner people knew their lines and could get "off book," as they called it, the happier Phillip was with their work. My scene was scheduled for tomorrow's evening rehearsal and I wanted to be off book from the very beginning.

At dinner that night, everybody was talking about the costume shop mystery. Tad was there, sucking up one forkful of spaghetti after another, so nobody actually used the word *ghost*. But it was clear what they thought. I'd been thinking about the way the idea of this ghost was growing when someone mentioned that Phyllis had found the costumes all laid out across the cutting table.

"They'd been hanging on the clothes rack when she left," Joan was saying when I tuned in, "and when she got back, the iron was plugged in, turned on high, and the costumes were lined up on the table as if somebody was getting ready to press them. She said the first thing she thought about was that old children's story—about the elves and the shoemaker. It was as if somebody had been meaning to help her."

I hadn't touched any costumes.

"Mischievous 'elves' they were, though," Toni

said. "They pulled the thread out of the sewing machines."

George, his mouth full, humphed.

"And dumped the trash can, too," Joan said. "Phyllis found the trash in a big pile on the floor."

"And the spools of thread on top of the pile."

Tad had stopped slurping up spaghetti noodles and was looking from Joan to Toni. "I thought Jared did it," he said, his voice squeaking. "Because my Jeep was missing."

"I never touched the costumes!" I overrode what he was saying with the exact truth.

"When I went to look for my Jeep, Hamlet wouldn't go into the little dressing room. I couldn't get him to go anywhere near it."

"Smart dog," George said.

Julia picked up a platter of garlic bread that was sitting on the table in front of her. "Who wants seconds? Garlic's great for what ails you." She put a piece on Tad's plate and passed the platter. "Tomorrow is put-in," she said to Phillip. "How soon before we'll be able to rehearse on the set?"

"First of the week, I hope," Phillip said, and the conversation drifted away.

I sat looking at Tad. He looked up at me and made a face. But his eyes gave him away. He was scared. Somebody besides me is playing practical jokes, I thought. I glanced at George, who had started the whole ghost thing in the first place. It had to be him.

That night, Tad wasn't at stage combat class. Hamlet got upset when he thought Tad was in danger, so he couldn't go along. And Tad wouldn't go without him. I was glad. Kent helped me with my fencing a lot, but it was still a good thing none of it was real. I got in one touch to every ten of Kent's, it seemed. I wanted to get a whole lot better before I started fencing with Tad.

The next morning, I was drafted to help the technical crew with the "load-in," which was what they called moving the set pieces that had been built in the college's scene shop from the truck onto the stage. It was a big job. Tad and Hamlet stayed in the costume shop, out of the way. It was amazing how Tad managed to avoid anything that looked like work. He still hadn't even gotten his stuff up off the floor of our room. I'd finally kicked a path clear from the door and shoved everything from my side over to his so there was at least a little bare rug by my bed. Neither Julia nor Phillip had been in our room lately, so they hadn't noticed. As far as I could tell, they'd forgotten all about it.

Unloading the truck was heavy work. The air conditioning in the theatre had been turned on, but even so, I was soaked with sweat in no time. The set was mostly platforms and walls that had been built in pieces as big as could be fit onto the truck and brought through the back doors of the theatre to the stage. Step units and ramps were going to connect the platforms to each other and the stage floor, and those had already been built, too. Onstage, all that had to be done was to attach the legs to the platforms and screw all the pieces together. That was the part Julia had called "put-in," for putting the set in place on the stage.

I was surrounded suddenly with a whole lot of new people, some of them technical members of the company, some students at the college. Except for the technical director—an intense guy named Joe, with a voice like nails against a blackboard—they seemed to be easygoing and friendly. And none of them knew anything about a ghost. It occurred to me that I might be able to change that. They'd be working on the stage, so I started thinking about how I could use the traps.

When the truck was finally empty and the stage was stacked high with platforms and wall units and lumber, Joe unrolled a floor plan and started hollering about finding the right legs for the right platforms. "They're all precut and numbered!" he said. "If you don't get the right ones in the right places, none of this is going to work." I sat on the arm of a seat in the front row and watched. A tall, skinny girl in black overalls and a chunky guy in holey blue jeans began screwing legs to platforms. They used screw guns that were plugged into an extension cord that ran to one of the electrical outlets sunk into the stage floor. Joe called the outlets "floor pockets." After watching awhile, I slipped away.

Down in the Trap Room, I listened to the sounds over my head and did my best to remember exactly where platforms had been placed. The first to get its legs was a low one, just a few inches higher than the stage floor. Joe had ordered that one set downstage right. If I opened a trapdoor under that platform, nobody would be able to see either the opening it made in the stage floor or me peeking out of it. And the floor pocket they were using was right at the edge of it.

Standing on a wooden box, I unlatched the trapdoor that seemed to me to be in the right place. The slight squeak was more than covered by the sounds of the screw guns and the voices of people calling to each other to hold this or get that. I'd gotten the right one—I was under the platform, and there was just room to get my head up through the trap. I could see people's feet and the orange extension cord snaking across the stage and down into the outlet only a few inches from me. Someone knelt down in front of me. I ducked back down. If the person happened to look underneath, we would have been practically nose-to-nose. But he was only screwing a ramp in place. A few minutes later, he got up and moved away. I waited till Joe called everybody upstage to help set one of the higher platforms onto its legs, then shot my hand out from under the platform and pulled loose the plug.

It took a while before anybody noticed. "Hey!" I heard finally. "What's the matter with this stupid screw gun? It was working a minute ago."

"This one, too!" somebody else shouted. "Check the extension cord."

A pair of feet approached. "It just pulled loose, that's all!" A hand reached down and plugged the cord in. I waited, listening to the sounds of the drills. Then, when Joe started hollering again and I figured everybody would be looking at him, I pulled the plug. This time, the screw guns were working when I did it, and they stopped suddenly. "Somebody check the damn plug again!"

The same pair of raggedy Nikes came and stood by the outlet. "How'd that happen? Hey, Jen, did you pull on this?"

"Nah. It's plenty long enough to reach."

"Must be the outlet." A pudgy hand reached down and plugged the cord in. Then it pulled the plug out. "It doesn't feel loose." The hand plugged the cord into first one and then the other of the two outlets and pulled it out again. "They're both tight enough. Good and tight! Weird." The hand plugged the cord in, tugged gently, and disappeared. "Okay, that ought to do it. Just don't pull on it, okay?"

"I didn't!" came the answer, over the sound of a screw gun.

The Nikes stood there awhile, and I imagined the person staring down at the outlets, wondering. When the shoes moved away, I waited till the other screw gun began, checked to be sure there was no one near, and pulled the plug again.

In the sudden silence, there were curses and the sound of a screw gun being slammed down against a platform. This time, the Nikes came fast and the hand snatched the cord. "Bloody poltergeists!" the voice said. "What's the matter with this thing? It's like it jumped out all by itself."

"Just plug it in somewhere else!" Joe yelled. "We haven't got time to mess around. I want to get all the platforms up and the facings on before we break for lunch!"

This time, the extension cord was plugged into a pocket in the middle of the stage, where I didn't dare open a trap. But watching those Nikes had given me another idea. When I heard another platform being set in place a little farther upstage and toward the center, I moved my box beneath the closest trapdoor and opened it. The platform above my head this time was higher, but I still couldn't be seen unless someone got right down on the floor and looked under. I got my head and both shoulders through the trap and waited. After a while, just as I'd hoped, a pair of canvas sneakers approached and a stair unit was shoved up against the platform. Then the Nikes came over, and the two people stood on either side of the stair unit and began screwing it to the platform. As the screw guns roared above my head, I untied the laces of the Nikes as gently and carefully as I could and then knotted them together. Quickly, I did the same to the sneakers and then dropped back down, latching the trapdoor closed. I didn't wait around to hear the result of what I'd done. I put the box back into the pile of junk hiding my lair and hurried up to the second floor. As casually as I could, I settled myself to watch the rest of the morning rehearsal.

On the way home in the van that evening, the talk was all about the ghost. And it didn't stop at dinner, even though Tad was at the table. Even the doubters had to admit that something very weird was going on. I'd been wondering if I'd be able to pretend I was hearing the story for the first time, but I didn't need to worry. It had grown. To hear Toni and Kent tell it, none of the power tools had stayed plugged in for more than a few minutes at a time all day, and the tech crew had been dropping like flies because their shoelaces were tied together. The girl named Jen, a volunteer from the college, got so upset when her laces got tied together the second time, she quit. My eyes were probably as wide by now as Tad's. *The second time?*

"I suppose you think that was all the work of your kindly, caretaking ghost," George said. "Helping out."

"Perhaps he's a purist," Joan suggested. "Perhaps power tools offend his sense of theatrical craftsmanship."

"So what does he have against sneakers?"

Tad's face was pink now, his eyes bulging. "I don't like ghosts. I'm not going back there." At the sound of his voice, Hamlet, who'd been lying at his feet, sat up. Tad grabbed at his collar. "Not even with Hamlet."

Phillip set down his knife and fork. "Of course you're going back. We're rehearsing your scenes this evening."

Tears began sliding down Tad's cheeks. "I'm not going back there. You can't make me!"

"For heaven's sake, Theodore, nobody saw a thing. Besides, if there is a ghost—"

Julia raised her hands as if to put them over Tad's ears, then dropped them again. She glared across the table. "Don't be ridiculous, Phillip! There's no such thing as a *ghost*."

"All I'm saying is that if there *is* one, it's a disembodied spirit. Disembodied! It can't hurt anybody, for heaven's sake."

"Somebody could have gotten hurt when they fell!" Tad was holding Hamlet against his leg as if the dog were some kind of antighost weapon. Hamlet licked his face.

"Nobody did."

"I don't care. I'm not going back there."

"You most certainly are," Phillip said, and his voice was like cold steel.

"This is ridiculous! There is *no* ghost at the Addison Opera House." Julia looked around the table. "Grow up. All of you. Someone is playing practical jokes, and it's time to find out who and put an end to it." She patted Tad's arm and sighed. "I ought to be working on publicity material tonight,

81

but I'll go to rehearsal with you instead. I'll stay right there with you every minute. No 'ghost' will tie your shoelaces together, I promise! All right?"

Tad didn't say anything. He just sat there, gripping Hamlet's collar.

"All right?"

He nodded finally, but you didn't have to be a mind reader to know he didn't think it was all right at all.

A piece of me felt like laughing right out loud.

CHAPTER
TEN

What I'd been dreading for weeks, worrying about, trying to get ready for, was finally about to happen. My first rehearsal. My throat hurt and I seemed to be having trouble breathing. I wasn't sure I'd even be able to talk. I was standing at the edge of the taped stage floor, waiting to be told what to do and trying to make myself feel like a crown prince, next in line to the throne, when Julia came in with Tad and settled herself on a chair next to the stage manager's table, her long tanned legs stretched out in front of her. She pushed her hair off the back of her neck with both arms and held it up as she said something to Toni about the humidity outside. As hard as I'd worked memorizing my lines, every word I'd learned went right out of my head.

As it turned out, it didn't matter, because Tad's

and my scenes, which hadn't been done before, had to be blocked first. That meant that everyone had to carry their scripts anyway so they could write in them where they were supposed to go and what they were supposed to do. Tad had a scene first, with Joan and a woman from Addison who was playing the part of the old queen. That was the last scene of act 2. My first scene was the first scene of act 3. I sat on the floor, leaned against the wall, and avoided looking at Julia. For some reason every time I did, my stomach knotted with a cold certainty that I was about to make a complete fool of myself.

As scared as he had been about the ghost, Tad seemed totally relaxed as they worked their way through his scene. Easy enough for him—he'd done this all his life. He was so sure of himself, he didn't even write down what he was supposed to do. I couldn't stand to watch. At least it didn't look like he'd memorized his lines.

I closed my eyes and tried going over my lines. It came to me how weird a coincidence the end of the scene was, given what was going on at the theatre. Richard is about to send both princes off to the Tower, and Tad's character says he doesn't want to go there because that's where his uncle Clarence died and he's afraid of his ghost. Shakespeare might have written Tad's line especially for him.

When Tad's scene was done, Toni called, "Act three, scene one—a planetary surface road," and it was time for me to begin. Tad didn't come on till

84

later in the scene, so he had gone to sit next to Julia, and I avoided looking at either of them as I moved where Phillip directed me to move, and made notes in my script. Nobody was acting at this point, not even Phillip—they were just moving to where they were supposed to deliver a line and saying it. When we got to the place where Tad came on and he and I were supposed to greet each other, he was—very obviously—holding his script with his middle finger sticking up. Suddenly, I had an idea about these two princes that I hadn't thought of before. Maybe they didn't like each other any better than Tad and I did.

When we were finished blocking the scene, Phillip gave us a five-minute break before we ran it again and came over to talk to me. "I just want to give you something to think about before you start," he said. "One way to get into your character is to find something in you that's like him. See if you can find some feelings that match what your character feels. Some experiences in your life that are like his in some way. No matter what role you play, you can always find something of that character in yourself. That's how you make him real to an audience." He patted me on the shoulder. "And Jared—relax."

Easy for him to say, I thought. I considered my character. He was a kid who had always known that someday he would be the king. And everybody else knew it, too. So they would have bowed and scraped to him all his life, trying to stay on his good side for when he came into power. It would be easy, living like that, to grow up thinking the whole world revolved around you. Just like Tad. There wasn't any piece of me that felt like that. I decided, at least for now, to try to imagine how Tad felt.

When Toni called, "Places," I put my script down. I thought about Tad, the way he had looked at me the first time he saw me, as if I were a bug that had crawled in when somebody opened the screen door. Or when he lit that cigarette in the dressing room, daring me to say anything about it to anyone. Tad, the crown prince.

As we began, almost from the moment Toni said, "Three, one—a planetary surface road," every bit of my nervousness just evaporated. Like magic. Everybody watching evaporated, too, and even the rehearsal hall itself. It was as if I had really become the prince. The king, my father, had died, and I was the older brother. The one about to be crowned king. The one with all the power. The lines came back to me. I felt taller. Stronger. And really grumpy that I'd had such a tiring trip trekking halfway across the planet for my coronation, and only one of my uncles had come out to greet me. Why should I, just about to become king, have to put up with that sort of disrespect?

Later, when Tad entered, my line was, "Richard of York, how fares our loving brother?" I found myself giving those last two words a trace of a sneer. And Tad, even though he was still having to read his lines, reacted. He made it perfectly clear how little he liked having to call me "dread lord." All the rest of the way through the scene, there was that edge of rivalry—two brothers who knew exactly what was what now that their father was gone. The words we said were all about royal manners, but underneath there was the knowledge that I was the one who would be king and—because I was there first—there was nothing he could do about it.

At the end of the scene when Tad said he was afraid of Clarence's ghost, it was easy to believe him. He had the same look in his eyes that he'd had at the dinner table.

And as I looked into Phillip's face, transformed now into the face of Richard, the scheming Duke of Gloucester, I understood suddenly how fragile my character's power really was. What could a ghost do to me in comparison to what Richard could? "I fear no uncles dead," I said.

"Nor none that live, I hope." The Duke of Gloucester smiled, but there was ice in his eyes.

"An if they live, I hope I need not fear." As I said it, I knew suddenly that this prince, no matter how spoiled and arrogant, knew he was in terrible danger. All he could do was put on a brave face. "But come, my lord, and with a heavy heart, thinking on them, go I unto the Tower." Walking between my two guards, I felt sure my character understood now that he would never be king. This was his last chance to look as if he could be.

As I left the stage, Toni and the other actors—

even Julia, even Phillip—applauded. The spell was broken suddenly, and I was Jared again. Jared, who hadn't made a fool of himself after all.

"I thought you'd never acted before," Phillip said.

I shook my head. "I haven't."

Toni nodded. "I told you it was in the genes!"

Tad scowled as he sat down next to Julia. But Julia, nodding, smiled at me.

During the break, Phillip sat by me and asked how I liked his *Star Wars* idea. I said it was a good idea. Then I told him I'd been thinking how funny it would be to do it really like *Star Wars*, using the characters from the movie as the characters in the play.

"You mean like Darth Vader as Richard?"

I shook my head. "I think the emperor would be Richard—he had the real power."

"Then who would Darth Vader be?" Julia asked.

"Buckingham," I said. "Richard's henchman. The one who does his dirty work."

"What about Luke Skywalker?" Phillip asked. "Who would he be?"

I grinned. I had thought the whole thing out down in my hideout the day before when I'd been practicing my lines. All the characters in the play could be played by somebody from *Star Wars*. "Luke would be Richmond. The good guy who beats Richard in the end. And Princess Leia would be Lady Anne."

Julia made a face. "I refuse to wear my hair that way—like bagels over my ears."

Others had gathered around us. Kent wanted to know who R2-D2 and C-3PO would be.

"Catesby and Ratcliffe."

"Lando Calrissian?" Laurence asked.

"Stanley."

"What about Han Solo?" Toni said. "I just *love* Harrison Ford."

"Han Solo would be Hastings," I answered. "When Richard wants to get rid of him, instead of 'Off with his head!' he could say 'Encase him in carbonite!'"

"That's it!" Phillip said, becoming Richard to say the whole line. "Encase him in carbonite! Now by St. Paul I swear I will not dine until I see the same."

Everybody laughed. Everybody except Tad, who sat next to Julia, snapping his gum and glaring at me.

CHAPTER ELEVEN

There was more than an hour of rehearsal before we would be going home. Now that our scene was over and they were on to the next, there was nothing for Tad or me to do. Tad, still scowling, stomped down to the costume shop, Julia following with her folder of publicity materials to work on. Nobody was paying any attention to me, so I slipped out and went down to my hideout. I lit the lamp and curled up in my chair to think about what had just happened. First there had been that sense of becoming somebody else. Not like pretending, but as if I had really quit being me for a while. I liked it. More than liked it. For just that little while, Jared Kingsley and all the junk of Jared Kingsley's real life had disappeared. Like magic.

Besides that, there was the applause. What a

sound that was. Even Phillip had applauded. And Julia.

Was this how Serena felt? I wanted to feel like that again. It was like getting off the Beast at Kings Island, wishing you could just turn around and get right back on. I wanted that feeling again!

The Prince of Wales was a little part, just that one scene and the one where the princes come back as ghosts. Plus the pantomime of when the princes get smothered in their beds. Shakespeare didn't show them being murdered onstage, but Phillip was putting the scene in. He said it was too dramatic to leave out.

It wasn't much, this role. But it felt like the beginning of something important. Really important. As if my life were starting all over again. I thought about what Toni had said—that I would make a good Puck in *A Midsummer Night's Dream*. I wondered if there was a copy around that I could read. Or—what was the other one? *The Tempest?*

All of a sudden, I realized that for the first time since I'd come to Addison, Michigan, I wasn't just surviving. I felt good. I felt wonderful!

I pushed myself up from the chair and settled into fencing posture, holding an imaginary foil in my hand. *"En garde!"* I said to an invisible foe. With a lunge and a lightning-fast strike, I ran him through and turned to face my next opponent, who was about to leap at me from behind the chair.

And noticed a wooden chest under the pedestal table. Where had it come from? And who had put it there? Someone had been in my hideout. I looked carefully around. Nothing else seemed different from the last time I'd been here.

The chest was shaped like an old-fashioned steamer trunk, only smaller, with metal bands around it and a hasp that could be locked with a padlock. There wasn't any padlock, though.

I dragged it out and knelt beside it. I brushed the dust from my hands and then looked more carefully. Dust lay thick on the top, on the handles, everywhere. The only disturbance in the dust was where I had grasped one handle to pull the chest out. Except for that it looked as if nothing and no one had touched the chest in a hundred years. How could that be?

I shook away the question. It couldn't be. Someone had brought it in here, probably dragging it by that handle. But why? And what was in it?

The hasp was stiff and hard to lift, but I got the lid open. There was a sheet of yellowed paper on the top. I picked it up and it crumbled in my hands, sending paper crumbs and a cloud of dust drifting in the lamplight. Underneath was something that looked like a cross between a poster and a theatre program.

It was a long, narrow sheet of paper covered with print, some tiny, some large. This paper was heavy and still almost white—nothing like the sheet that had crumbled. I lifted it as gently as I could and held it closer to the light.

BURTON'S

NEW THEATRE BROADWAY
OPPOSITE BOND STREET

STAGE MANAGER................MR. JOHN MOORE
ACTING MANAGER.............MR. WAYNE OLWINE

MR.
GARRICK MARSDEN

WHO HAS BEEN UNANIMOUSLY PRONOUNCED BY THE
PRESS OF NEW YORK TO BE THE GREATEST ACTOR
ENGLAND HAS SENT TO NEW YORK IN MANY A YEAR
WILL APPEAR IN SHAKESPEARE'S TRAGEDY, ADAPTED
BY COLLEY CIBBER, OF

RICHARD III

OR THE
BATTLE OF BOSWORTH FIELD

WHICH WILL BE PRESENTED IN A SUPERIOR MANNER
AND OWING TO THE LIMITED ENGAGEMENT CANNOT
BE REPEATED.

MISS FANNY MORANT
AS QUEEN ELIZABETH

MISS ADA CLIFTON
AS LADY ANNE

WEDNESDAY, JANUARY 5, 1859

The whole rest of the cast was listed in tiny print. Beneath that it said, "Every necessary Adjunct of Appropriate Scenery and Magnificent Costume and Properties will attend the performance of the piece."

At the bottom of the page were the ticket prices: "Dress Circles and Parquette Fifty Cents, Third Tier Twenty-five Cents, Orchestra or Stall Chairs One Dollar, and Balcony Chairs Seventy-five Cents."

Incredible coincidence, I thought. *Richard III*, done in 1859. Almost a century and a half ago! Underneath, there were more—for other plays. And there were some sturdier pieces that looked like advertising posters. They had pictures and much less printing. The pictures weren't photographs; they were drawings—of the leading man in costume. The plays they advertised were all different, at different theatres, but the leading man was the same in all of them—Garrick Marsden.

I looked through them, handling them as carefully as I could. The dates ranged from 1858 to 1887, with nothing between 1861 and 1865. Social studies came back to me. Eighteen sixty-one to 1865—the Civil War. An English actor would probably have gone home to avoid getting caught up in the fighting. There were two posters for *Macbeth*, one for a theatre in New York and the other for one in Pennsylvania. The last was for a play called *The Lost Is Found* at the Addison Opera House, Addison, Michigan.

At the bottom of the chest was a scrapbook with a padded black velvet cover. The velvet was shiny in places, as if it had been handled a lot. In gold lettering on the front was the name again—Garrick Marsden. I set the posters on the rug and lifted the heavy book out of the chest. The first page was completely taken up by a photograph printed in brown tones on thick, heavy cardboard. The picture was of a dramatic-looking young man with a longish face, intense dark eyes, and dark hair curled over his forehead and around his ears. He was standing with one hand on the back of a chair, looking off to one side, away from the camera. His expression was very serious. He wore a kind of tight jacket with long sleeves and a ruff of lace at the neck, a short skirt, and heavy tights. Garrick Marsden in costume.

I began turning pages. On some there were more handbills; on some there were newspaper clippings, printed on much heavier paper than newspapers use now. Some of the clippings advertised Garrick Marsden's Acting Company and some were reviews of the performances. I stopped to read an especially long one of a play called *The Ticket of Leave Man*. "Much as we have heard in praise of Mr. Marsden and his company," it began, "the reality far exceeded our expectations. His Robert Brierly was a masterpiece, natural and truthful, presenting a vivid portrait of the unfortunate 'Lancashire Lad.' We are indeed blessed to have this first class troupe, late of London and New York, visit our city to adorn the stage of our fine new hall." It was just the sort of review Serena would have had blown up and framed.

There were other reviews that were almost as good. Some of them didn't like some actor or another, or picked at the play, but every one was a rave about Garrick Marsden. One reviewer called him "the greatest tragedian currently traveling to the theatres of the West."

I was just about to turn the page from reading that review when I felt a draft across the back of my neck. Except there couldn't have been a draft. The door was closed, the traps were all closed, and the lamp flame hadn't even so much as flickered. I reached up and touched my neck. And felt the sensation again, only this time it wasn't just on my neck. This time, it was everywhere. And it wasn't like a draft. I was cold *inside*. As if the chill that had started on my skin was working its way into my bones.

I found myself gasping for breath then, the way I would if I'd been underwater too long and had just made it to the surface. My chest heaved as I struggled to get enough air. It felt like the oxygen was being sucked out of the room. What was happening to me?

"The notice is a trifle overwrought, of course."

The voice came from behind, and startled me so badly, the scrapbook fell off my lap onto the rug. I swiveled around and found myself staring up at a man sitting in the overstuffed chair.

"But gratifying nevertheless."

Before I knew it, I had scrambled to my feet, pushed through the space between the junk and the wall, and was outside in the hall, shaking all over and leaning against the sliding door I had shoved closed behind me. I stood there for what seemed a very long time, my ear pressed against the door, listening. There was no sound. Of course there was no sound, I told myself. No one is in there. No one *could* be in there. No one could *possibly* be in there.

Finally, I pulled the door open a crack and peaked in. There was nothing to see, of course, except the empty Trap Room, the glow of the oil lamp reflected on the ceiling, along with the shadow of my junk barricade. I opened the door the rest of the way and stepped inside. Still no sound. I tiptoed toward the entrance to my hideout, one hand on my chest, as if that way I could keep my heart from jumping out. Finally, taking a deep breath and keeping one hand against the rough wall of the room for support, I went back in.

He was still there, sitting in my chair and looking up at me. "Wh-who are you?" I managed to squeak.

"Garrick Marsden," the man said, and smiled so that his heavy upward-curved mustache seemed to tilt even more sharply upward. "I should think you would have seen that for yourself. There are some rather fine likenesses in the playbills."

It was true that he looked like the actor in the posters. An older version of the man on the first page of the scrapbook. His body was a little heavier and his hair was going gray. Under his eyes, which were still very dark and intense, drooped dark pouches of skin. He was dressed in a black velvet jacket over a white shirt with a high, stiff collar and a white brocade vest. He had on a wide silver-and-black-striped tie. On his head, at a jaunty angle, he wore a black felt hat with a wide brim and a high, flat crown. Now he raised it with one hand. It made him look both lordly and expectant, as if he were taking a curtain call after a really good performance. Still keeping one hand against the wall, to stay in touch with good, solid reality, I nodded.

"H-h-how do you d-d-do," I stuttered.

"Very well, thank you, when you consider how long I've been dead."

The man adjusted his tie and I noticed the silver drama masks that pinned it in place.

"You're a...a..."

The man smiled again and put his hat back on, settling it perfectly at the same jaunty angle as before. "A ghost. Yes. And very glad to have actors back in my theatre, producing Shakespeare again. Richard! One of my favorite roles. Deliciously evil, that man. It has been a long, lonely wait, I don't mind telling you. The American theatre isn't what it used to be."

Chapter Twelve

The man did not look like a ghost. Not that I knew what ghosts looked like. I didn't even believe there were such things. But if there were, weren't they supposed to be transparent? Weren't they supposed to glow in the dark—or float? They didn't just sit there solidly in an armchair, chatting like a normal, real, *live* person. I must be dreaming, I thought. This was like some bad movie. I must have fallen asleep while I was looking at the scrapbook....

"No," Garrick Marsden said, as if I'd said it out loud. "You are not dreaming. You are fully awake and alert. Rather more alert than most people, since it is, in fact, quite easy for you to see me." He reached out one hand. "Here. You can touch me, as well."

I put my hand behind my back. Whatever this was, I didn't feel up to shaking hands with it.

"Perhaps later, when you've grown used to me."

No thanks, I thought. I didn't want to see this guy often enough to get used to him. "What are you doing here?"

"Here in this room, or here in the opera house, or here on earth, when I ought long ago to have passed to my heavenly reward?"

"Any of those! All of them."

The ghost settled himself deeper into the chair and fingered a gold chain that hung from a pocket in his vest. "Odd that while my clothes have remained the same since my unfortunate demise, my watch stopped approximately along with my heart, and I've never been able to make it go again. Do you have the time, may I ask?"

I glanced at my watch. A ghost wanted to know what time it was! "Nine-thirty-seven."

"Then I'd best keep this brief. Rehearsal, I believe, ends at ten. I am here just now because you called me."

I shook my head. "I didn't! I don't even believe—"

"Quite so. You don't believe in ghosts. You may have heard the saying that whether humans believe in Him has no effect on God. The same could be said here. Whether you believe in me or not, here I am. And you called me. Not intentionally, perhaps, but intention matters as little as belief. I'm rather surprised—and a bit disappointed—that you haven't noticed what I've done for you."

"Done? For me?"

"The little touches I added to the tricks you've been perpetrating on the company."

I thought of the clothes laid out on the ironing board. Jen's shoelaces.

"As to the other questions—I remain at the opera house to watch over it and its actors, much as the Man in Gray watches over the Theatre Royal. You've heard of—"

"Yes. Joan says she's seen him."

The ghost nodded. "I saw him as well, in 1863, when I was performing *Hamlet*."

"He was there then?"

"Of course. The Man in Gray has been appearing at the Royal since the eighteenth century. His appearance, they say, assures a success. It was true with my *Hamlet*. Only the most sensitive, however, have seen him." The ghost stared at me very hard, his thick eyebrows nearly meeting between his heavy-lidded eyes. I felt my ears going hot. "You, I feel certain, would see him readily. It's what will make you a fine actor."

"Me?"

"Certainly. Don't deny that you've felt it. I've been watching you. You have sensitivity, imagination, passion. You are destined for greatness upon the stage." The ghost shuddered. "Assuming that in this decadent age there is room for greatness." He smoothed his mustache and sighed. "How could I have foreseen, when I chose to watch over this theatre, the coming of that stage abomination, vaudeville?" He shuddered. "Or, worse yet, moving pictures? I cannot imagine why an audience would attend a moving-picture performance—always the same, day after day, night after night. No spark between audience and actor. No chance to see a sublimely memorable performance—or a disaster. One might as well read a book. At least with a book, though the pages remain the same, one's own imagination has room to create! I spent almost seventy long, lonely years hiding out in a dressing room to avoid the moving pictures." He gestured toward the rug. "Don't just stand there looking uncomfortable, boy. Sit down."

Reluctantly, I moved away from the wall and sat at the edge of the rug, as far from the chair as I could manage to be. "What about the other question? Why didn't you go to heaven when you died?" I had considered mentioning the other place, but I didn't know how easily a ghost might be offended. Or what such a solid-looking ghost could do if it was. "Disembodied," Phillip had said. Not this one!

Marsden sighed again. "There is an eternity to be dead. And I didn't relish the idea of spending it drifting down golden streets playing a harp."

"That isn't really what it's like—is it?"

"How would I know? I never went. I am an actor! A man of the theatre. How could I give that up?"

"If you're really a ghost—"

"If? What else could I be?"

I shrugged. "I don't know. A dream maybe. A hallucination. But if someone who dies can stick around and appear to people, talk to them—"

"Not an easy thing, appearing. Let alone talking. It took me quite awhile to get the knack of it."

"But if someone *can*, then why doesn't everybody?"

"It takes a grand passion. A passion larger than life itself. Larger than death! Few people have the capacity for such a passion. My passion is for the theatre, of course."

"How...uh..." I didn't know how to ask my question. "How did you—"

"Die? It's quite all right. I have never cared for euphemisms—*passed over* and so on. It was a rather ignominious way to go, I'm sorry to say. Sandbag."

"What?"

"Sandbag. They were used as counterbalances for the drop curtains. One broke loose during a performance of *The Lost Is Found*. I happened to be in the wrong place. It was over in an instant." The ghost took off his hat and held it over his heart. "May I rest in peace."

"I'm sorry."

He waved his hat in the air and smiled. "Don't be. Rather a good end for an actor, really. To die onstage, at the height of my fame."

Marsden looked down at me, his eyes so intense,

it made me shiver. "I suppose you wonder why I was performing in a town as insignificant as Addison, Michigan, in the first place. After all, I had played the finest theatres of New York and London, appeared before the crowned heads of Europe."

He was sounding like his advertising.

"Struck down by a good deed, I was. Ironic, don't you think?" The ghost ran his hand through his hair and put his hat back on. His face, already creased and lined, seemed to sag with unhappy memory. I thought I saw tears gathering in his eyes.

"An old friend, a company manager—what you might call a director these days—lost his lead actor just two months before the end of his season. Booked solid, he was. Not that his company was any good—none of them could act worth a tinker's dam. A third-rate company altogether. But out here in the country, audiences barely knew the difference. They came to twenty different *Uncle Tom* companies a season and every threadbare *Our American Cousin*—just because Lincoln was shot while watching it—but they would hardly cross the street for Shakespeare. *The Lost Is Found* was about as deep a drama as they could handle, and that's what Edward gave them. Cheap performers and surefire plays. What he lacked in theatrical integrity, Edward made up for in shrewdness. As a favor, I agreed to play the leading role for a few performances—just to keep him from losing the bookings. If they had had to cancel, they'd have been stranded out here in the hinterlands with no money to get back to New York. So, my good deed has resulted in my spending eternity at the Addison Opera House."

"Not quite the Theatre Royal," I said.

The ghost shook his head sadly. Then he brightened. "It was new then. Quite nicely appointed, for a western house. I could have done worse. And I became quite well known among the touring companies later." He sat up very straight and made a sweeping gesture with one arm, as if he were about to take a bow. "I became a legend, while the road endured. I saved many a minor actor's reputation, whispering lines in their ears, retrieving lost or forgotten props, even prodding them from their dressing rooms to keep them from missing an entrance!

"And once I stopped a disgruntled stagehand from setting fire to the place. The manager had refused to pay him for the time he spent down here in this very room lost in a bottle instead of tending to his cues. Somewhere in the dark corners, you may find some empty bottles still. That sot had no imagination whatsoever. I was as invisible to him as a summer breeze. You should have seen his face when I kept blowing out his matches." The ghost paused in reverie. Then, with a start, he brought himself back.

"As long as there were performers, I was here to help. Even, I'm chagrined to say, the vaudevillians. I would be remembered still if the moving pictures had not driven the living theatre out of existence."

"So that's what you want to do now? Help?"

"Of course! This company—and you in particular. You remind me of myself. The same passion. The same spark of real talent I had at your age, the same strength and determination. And"—this time, the ghost's gaze made me squirm; it made me feel as if he were looking right through me—"I see as well that you have sustained a deep hurt. An abandonment that is a wound to the heart. It will, if you can survive it, lead not merely to success but on, as I say, to greatness. Only such a wound can give one the understanding, the pathway to the souls of the towering characters—heroes and villains alike. Ah, yes—villains. You may one day far outshine your father as Richard."

The ghost rubbed his hands together. "How I've longed for a time when the hall would be alight again, greasepaint in the dressing rooms, footlights lit. Your father brings to life a dream I scarcely dared to dream, that the Bard's immortal lines might be heard once more from this very stage. Perhaps audiences are hungry at last for high drama and great tragedy."

"Don't count on it," I told him, remembering the arguments about whether the theatre could survive. "The big question is still whether anyone will actually come."

"They will come. *Richard the Third* is a charm."

"A charm?"

"It has a splendid history." The ghost patted his

watch chain again. "Time does not dim its power. It was performed in 1750 in New York, in the first professional theatrical season in that city. And you know what New York has been to the American theatre ever since. *Richard* was the play the great Edmund Kean chose for his Broadway debut in 1820. And it was my own first major Shakespearean role. I played it four times in London and once in New York. Even, once, on tour. People can't get enough of Richard—there is something forever compelling about a man who revels in his own evil. What begins with *Richard the Third* is guaranteed success."

"My father will be glad to hear that."

"No doubt that's why he chose it. When the cast learns that I am here, watching over their production, they will be certain to create a masterpiece."

"Not everybody believes—"

The ghost smiled broadly. "The sensitive ones—the imaginative ones—will, from time to time, see me. Hear me. Feel me. And the other ones will see evidence of my presence. They will believe."

"Some of them might be afraid of you."

Marsden stood up then, and I couldn't help but cower back, away from him. Goose bumps rose along my arms. As solid and normal as Marsden looked while sitting in the chair, there was something in his presence, standing, that was rather scarily more vivid. I had that feeling again, the chill that seemed to go right to the middle of me. There seemed to be a dimming of light that had nothing to do with the lamp. For the first time, I was certain this was real. I was not dreaming.

When Marsden spoke again, his voice was so penetrating that I thought everyone in the building must surely be able to hear it. His eyes flashed. Gone was the quaint, old-fashioned, friendly helper. Now I could imagine this man playing the role of Richard. "Whoever is afraid of me does not deserve to tread the boards!"

With that, Garrick Marsden, hat, mustache, velvet coat, and well-shined boots, began to shimmer, like water with a breeze blowing across it, against the dark background of the Trap Room wall. I had to struggle again to take a breath. The air had gone thin. Thin and cold. As I gasped for air, Marsden blinked out, suddenly, like a light. I was alone again.

CHAPTER THIRTEEN

It took awhile to catch my breath after Marsden disappeared. It felt as if the ghost had taken most of the air with him, wherever he went. And the heat, too. My teeth were positively chattering with cold.

And now that he was gone, I was downright excited. There really *was* a ghost, and I was the only person in the company who knew who he was and why he was here, the only one who had actually talked to him. It was almost as if Marsden belonged to me. I put the posters back in Marsden's chest and dragged it into a dark corner where it wouldn't be seen even if someone discovered my hideout. I wasn't ready to share him.

Then I remembered his scrapbook. I hadn't finished looking at it. When Marsden appeared, I wasn't even halfway through. But it wasn't on the floor where it should have been. I remembered that it had fallen off my lap when I turned and found him sitting in the chair. It should have been right there. I looked under the chair. No scrapbook. I dragged out the chest and went through everything inside. It wasn't there.

It had to be somewhere. I searched the dark edges of the room. I found the empty liquor bottles Marsden had told me about and a wooden box covered with soot and dust, but no scrapbook. As I stood there, staring down at the box, I realized that neither Marsden's chest nor this box had been in the Trap Room when I fixed it up. I'd have seen them. The liquor bottles, too, for that matter. Marsden must have put all these things where I could find them. And now, for whatever reason, he'd taken his scrapbook back. Maybe so no one else could learn what he'd told me. I grinned to myself. At least for now, the real ghost of the Addison Opera House was my secret.

I sat down in the chair, pulled the box over, and opened it. Inside was another collection of theatre posters and handbills—all from plays that had been done at the Addison Opera House, from the 1850s through the turn of the century. I decided to take them to Phillip and see if we could make a historical bulletin board for the lobby. One of them, I saw, was for *The Lost Is Found*, the play that had been Marsden's final performance. I leaned back, holding the handbill announcing the exclusive engagement of the star of the New York and European stage, Garrick Marsden. The face of the man who only minutes before had been sitting in this very chair stared up at me.

I went back over everything he'd told me. I had "called" him, he said. But how? And why? It didn't make sense. I hadn't even known he was here. And then there was the rest of it. About me being destined for greatness on the stage—someday a better Richard than Phillip Kingsley. A week ago, even two days ago, that wouldn't have meant a thing to me. Now, suddenly, I could feel my heart beating faster just thinking about it. A better Richard than Phillip Kingsley!

I closed my eyes, picturing the scene—me in a tuxedo in front of a microphone, accepting a Tony Award for Best Actor. I imagined myself holding up the trophy, looking past the television cameras, past the audience, past Serena, crying and applauding from the front row. "This is for you, Pop!" And then looking down again. The audience standing, applauding wildly. Next to Serena in the front row, Phillip and Julia Kingsley—Julia smiling at me the way she'd smiled at rehearsal. And next to them, Tad in a stained and rumpled tux, chewing gum, his hands unmoving at his sides. I saw myself bowing. Smiling. And Tad raising one hand to flip me off.

I grinned then, thinking about Tad. A real ghost would just about scare him to death!

111

I took my tape player and a couple books down to my hideout the next morning and waited there, hoping Marsden would appear. By lunchtime, he hadn't shown, so I gave up. After lunch, I took the box of handbills and posters to show Phillip and he gave me the job of designing the lobby display. I worked in the lobby most of the afternoon, aware of the sounds of hammers and power tools coming from the stage, where the set was being worked on. Nobody, it seemed, was unplugging tools today.

I put the poster for *The Lost Is Found*, with the drawing of Garrick Marsden, in the center of the display. Nobody but Marsden and I would understand the significance of that particular production in the history of the Addison Opera House.

When I finished, I narrowly avoided running into Toni and George on their way down from the rehearsal room on break. I didn't want Toni to see me and think up some errand for me, so I ducked into the little dressing room. The door was kept propped open all the time, to air it out. George was complaining that his crossword puzzle had disappeared, and Toni was trying to convince him that he must have forgotten where he'd put it.

"I'm telling you, I know exactly where I left it," George was saying. "It was at my place in the dressing room and it's not there now. Everyone else was in the rehearsal hall. One of the techies must have taken it. Their idea of a prank, I suppose."

"I'll ask, but I can't imagine..."

As soon as they were gone, I scooted out of the little dressing room. No matter how long they left it to air out, it was still a nasty place. Down in my hideout, I lit the lamp and sat on the hassock, facing the big chair, and thought about Garrick Marsden. Would he show up again? And did I just have to wait till he did? Maybe, if I'd "called" him before, I could do it now. Literally. "Mr. Marsden?" I said, my voice sounding loud in my own ears. There were tech people working overhead. "Are you there? Here?" I said a little more quietly. "Mr. Marsden?"

Nothing. I waited, almost holding my breath. Would he come? After a few moments, the room dimmed, as if someone had turned down the lamp wick, though the flame was as high as ever. Now, as I tried to breathe, it felt again as if the oxygen was being sucked out of the room, and the familiar chill began. The air in front of the chair seemed to shimmer, distorting the edges of things. Marsden didn't blink on the way he had blinked out. It was more like a graphic appearing on a computer screen. At first, there was only a man-sized blur. Then, little by little, the form took on color and shape and definition.

As he grew more solid, I fought down the urge to get up and bolt from the room. His eyes seemed almost to be blazing, his mouth curved in a kind of sneer. But then he was fully there, fully real, and he smiled. I relaxed as his face settled into the expression I remembered, the friendly, chatty old actor. "You called?" Marsden said.

"I guess I did this time," I answered, and put my hands on my knees to keep them from shaking.

Marsden winked then and pulled a folded newspaper out of his coat. It was George's crossword puzzle. "Careless of him to leave this lying about."

"You took George's crossword puzzle?"

Marsden winked again and his mustache curved upward as he grinned. "He says such dreadful things about me!"

"I thought you said you were here to do good things for the theatre."

Marsden gave me a wounded look. "Just having a little fun. It's been a long, melancholy time here all by myself." He slipped the crossword puzzle back into his jacket. "Besides, there's a long and noble tradition of theatrical pranks. I didn't steal his puzzle, after all. I'm going to give it back." His eyes, which had looked so ferocious when he first appeared, got all twinkly. "Where do you think I should leave it for him? It should be somewhere no ordinary mortal could have put it. We'll give him a thing or two to think about. How about hanging from the *A* above the stage?"

"That wouldn't be any good. He already thinks one of the tech people took it—they'd have no trouble getting it up there."

Marsden frowned for a moment, and then he grinned. "Of course. It isn't *where* so much as *when*."

"What do you mean?"

He put a finger to his lips and looked mysterious.

"You'll see." He rubbed his hands together. "I played some wonderful pranks in my day."

"What sorts of pranks?"

Marsden looked off toward the ceiling, frowning as if he was sorting through his memories, nodding slightly when he found the one he wanted. "One tour, we were saddled with a dreadful actor. Not only did he have no sense of character, he forgot more lines than he remembered. The second show of the season, he was given a part so small it was more stage dressing than character. But that didn't help. The whole time he was onstage, he moved. He shifted from foot to foot, gazed out into the seats, twiddled with his costume. No one in the audience could look at anyone but him, fidgeting there. I was forced to make my own gestures ever broader and more dramatic to wrench the audience's attention away from him. Then he began to make sounds—actual sounds!—during my most important monologue. Sighs, hiccups. Finally one night, a loud and fruity belch. The climax of my monologue, of course, was lost in the ensuing merriment."

"So what did you do?"

"Near the end of the play, the man was onstage with the whole company as the climactic scene between the hero—myself—and the villain took place on a platform representing a mountain summit high above the stage. His single line—'Look there! The count approaches!'—signaled the beginning of the scene. In the intermission, I arranged with the company that when he said his line, everyone would leave the stage. Then neither the actor playing the villain nor I came on. He was left at center stage all alone, with no one to cover for him and nothing to say. He had what he wanted—the whole audience paying attention only to him.

"We watched from the wings, of course. A more terrified actor you never saw. I must say he made a valiant effort at first. Looked off one way, as if he expected someone to appear at any moment. Then off the other way. Even pointed to the empty platform where we were supposed to be, trying to get the audience to focus on something other than himself. There's nothing so ghastly as the feel of an audience that knows something is going wrong but can't tell exactly what. Even ghastlier is the moment when you know that *they* know that whatever's wrong, it's your fault. By the time he gave up and fled, he had turned bright scarlet and was shaking like a reed in a high wind.

"When he was gone, the rest of the cast came back on as if nothing had happened and finished the play. He didn't come back for the curtain call. We learned later that he caught the next train out of town. As far as I know, he never went on the stage again. 'A consummation devoutly to be wished.'" Marsden chuckled. "It was such a simple trick, really, and it worked so well!"

I chuckled with him. This was not just a care-taking ghost. He was a trickster, too!

CHAPTER FOURTEEN

When I got upstairs, rehearsal was just breaking up and George was standing at Toni's table, speaking loudly and angrily. "I was almost finished with it, and I want it back. I never leave a crossword unfinished—it's a point of honor!" The others, collecting water bottles, scripts, books, needlework and putting them into bags, duffels, and carryalls, didn't seem to be paying much attention. "I left it at my place in the dressing room and it vanished. The tech people say they don't know anything about it, so one of you must have it. Someone's trying to be funny." Clutching his leather bag under one arm, he drew himself up to his full height. "Well, I am not amused!"

"Perhaps you only thought you left it in the dressing room," Joan said. "Check your bag."

"I know precisely where I left it! Besides, I've checked my bag twice," he said. "It is not there!"

"Whatever you say," Joan said, smiling her grandmotherly smile. "Just a suggestion."

"All right, all right. I'll show you." George set his bag on the table and unzipped it. "If it were in here, I wouldn't have spent the whole afternoon—" He stopped and his face began to go red, the color moving upward from his neck. He reached into his bag and pulled out his crossword puzzle. I couldn't keep myself from laughing; everybody else was laughing, too. "Okay, now, I want to know what's going on here. I took everything out of this bag not five minutes ago—everything."

Toni nodded. "He did! And he did it down in the dressing room earlier, too. I'm a witness. It wasn't there."

"And now it is—right on the top. Where I couldn't have missed it!"

Phillip came over, jingling his car keys. "So where's the bag been since you last looked?"

George, his face still red, snatched up his bag and clutched it to his chest. "It's been with me! It was never farther from me than the next chair."

"You must have looked away just long enough for some joker to—"

"I did not! I'm telling you, it wasn't five minutes ago!"

Toni, her eyes wide, agreed with him. "It's completely impossible. Nobody went near it." I smothered another laugh, one hand over my mouth. This was what Marsden had meant by *when* rather than *where*. The others weren't laughing anymore. I looked around to see if I could tell where Marsden might be. I thought I detected a kind of shimmer in the air by the window, but I couldn't be sure.

"There has to be *some* explanation," Phillip said.

"A very simple one," Joan said, settling her knitting bag over her arm. "The ghost."

Julia left the room, shaking her head.

"I thought he was supposed to be looking after the theatre," Laurence said, "not playing pranks."

Joan patted George on the shoulder. "If I were you, I'd watch what I said about this ghost! You're lucky he has a sense of humor."

"Hey, Jared!" I turned, to see Kent putting on his motorcycle helmet. "I've got my extra helmet. You want a ride?"

"Sure!" I turned to Phillip. "Is that okay?"

"I don't see why not. Just be careful."

On the way, we passed Phillip and Julia's car, Tad and Hamlet in the backseat. Kent said Tad had never been allowed to ride with him. I waved. Tad flipped me off.

It was my night to set the table. Toni was making tuna casserole. As soon as it was in the oven, she told me, she could go outside for a cigarette or two. Then, when the casserole was nearly done, she'd cook some frozen veggies for balance. "George'll complain, but then, George complains about almost everything other people eat. He's the only one who never has to take a turn cooking, for fear he'd make us all eat alfalfa sprouts and tofu."

Kent, as usual, went into the living room, sprawled on the couch, and flipped on the television to watch whichever talk show had the rowdiest guests. Phillip and Julia arrived, and Tad, with Hamlet following, went up to our room, so I stayed with Kent until I couldn't stand listening to the bickering on the television anymore. I went out to the kitchen. Toni wasn't there, but the smell of the casserole was just beginning to make itself known.

Hamlet came down when I was just finishing setting the table, sniffed around the kitchen awhile, then settled onto the couch with Kent. Tad came a few minutes later and I heard him arguing with Kent about changing the channel. As I was leaving the kitchen, I heard a cartoon show theme song and knew Tad had won. "Prince" was right! Nobody in the company ever seemed willing to stand up to that kid.

Up in our room, I picked my way among the dirty clothes and toys that still littered the floor on Tad's side. I flung myself onto my futon and lay staring at the ceiling, thinking about Garrick Marsden and the trick he'd played on George. Suddenly, I became aware of a burned smell in the air. Like old matches. No—like burned paper. It must have been there all along, I realized, but it had taken awhile to connect with my brain. I sat up, sniffing. The metal wastebasket from next to Tad's desk was sitting on his futon, a pack of matches lying beside it. The trash—old Kleenexes and gum wrappers—had been dumped on the floor with the dirty clothes.

I went over to look. In the bottom was a mound of ash and a couple of charred bits of paper. I pulled one out. It was the corner of a photograph, mostly empty border, but with the tiniest bit of a brick building showing along the blackened edge. My stomach lurched and I turned to look at my dresser. The frame that held Pop's picture was facedown. I knew without looking that the bit I held in my hand was all that was left of the picture Mr. Steinmetz had taken of Pop on our fire escape with the white pigeon that used to come and land on his shoulder and beg to be fed. It was the only decent photograph I had of Pop—the old Pop. And now it was nothing but a pile of ash.

I looked at the ash pile again. It was too big to have been just the picture. What else had Tad destroyed? I scanned my half of the room and saw what I should have seen the minute I came in. He hadn't tried to hide anything. My boxes had been moved and restacked; the flaps of the top box were standing open. Still clutching the piece of Pop's picture, my heart beating in my throat, I went and looked in. My karate certificates, that Pop had always meant to have framed for me, were crumpled like old newspaper. My stamp album was under them. I didn't have to sort through the box to know what it was that had made that pile of ash. They had been on the very top—the *Playbill* from Serena's only ever Broadway show and her new eight-by-ten glossy publicity shot with her résumé on the back. She had left it with me before she went back to New York.

My hands, all by themselves, clenched into fists, squeezing so tight my knuckles went white and my fingernails bit into my palms. I plunged down the steps and into the living room, where Tad and Hamlet were stretched out on the couch. Kent had gone. I threw myself at Tad, pummeling him with both fists. He started to holler, and Hamlet jumped off the couch, barking. Tad wasn't quite the pushover I'd expected him to be. He fought back, using hands and feet, too, and we rolled off the couch onto the floor. I felt a tug as Hamlet got his teeth into the leg of my jeans and tried to drag me away. I was vaguely aware of the sounds of people converging on the living room, but I kept punching at Tad, trying to get a clear shot at his eye or his jaw as I did my best to avoid getting a fist in my own face.

"Enough! Stop that! Hamlet, let go." The tugging at my leg stopped and I felt myself being pulled to my feet by the back of my shirt. Phillip let go of my shirt and held me by both arms as Kent helped Tad to his feet.

"He attacked me!" Tad yelled. "I was just sitting here watching TV and he attacked me for no reason!"

Julia and Toni and Del had come in and everyone was looking at me, waiting for me to say something. I could hear the Road Runner's "beep-beep" as the television blared on.

"He destroyed my things," I said. "Pictures of Serena and Pop. Serena's Broadway *Playbill.*"

"Tad?" Phillip said.

"I don't know what he's talking about," Tad said.

"He did. I'll show you," I said.

"Take Hamlet outside, would you please?" Phillip said to Kent. Then he and Julia and Tad followed me upstairs, and I showed them the wastebasket, the ashes, the empty picture frame. Tad just stood there, his bottom lip stuck out, his arms crossed in front of his chest. "I didn't do that," he said again. "I don't know anything about it."

"I suppose you think I did it myself."

He shrugged. "Maybe you did. Maybe you wanted to get me in trouble."

"It's the only picture I have of my grandfather," I said. "I'd never do that!"

Tad rolled his eyes. "How do we even know that's what it was? All that's left is some ashes. They could have been anything!"

I lunged at him, and Phillip grabbed me by the shirt again. "Enough!"

Julia picked up the book of matches. "Whatever happened, whoever did this, it was a very dangerous thing to burn paper in here."

"He did it!" I said, knowing even as I said it how

123

hopeless it was. I couldn't prove a thing. "While I was setting the table, he did it."

Phillip let go of my shirt and looked from me to Tad. "I don't know who did what. All I know is that we don't have the time or the energy for this nonsense. We have a theatre to open. No one has time to play referee for the two of you. You are going to have to work it out between yourselves." He looked around the room. "I thought you were told to clean this mess up, Tad."

Julia sighed. "He's been told and told."

"All right, then. Tad, you will deal with the mess before you come down to dinner. Do you understand?" Tad nodded, his lip still stuck out, his eyes sullen. "And this time, we'll check to make sure you've done it."

Then Phillip turned to me. "As for you, Jared— if you have a problem, you bring it to one of us. And if the two of you must fight, you'll do it in a controlled situation under Laurence's supervision. A couple of good fencing matches ought to use up a little of this energy."

"We're not asking much of either of you," Julia said. "Just that you behave decently to each other and refrain from adding to the stress of an already-stressful situation. Is that too much to ask?"

"Is it?" Phillip said. Tad and I both shook our heads. "We had hoped that this would be a good experience, for both of you. But we can't make it happen. If you can't get along with each other, at least stay out of each other's way!"

"Whichever of you did this," Julia said, gesturing at the wastebasket with the book of matches and then putting them into her pocket, "there's to be no more playing with fire. I don't want to see anything like this ever again."

Phillip wants me to stay out of Tad's way, I thought as Phillip and Julia shepherded me out of the room. All right. I'd just do that. I'd let Garrick Marsden deal with Tad.

CHAPTER FIFTEEN

When I got down to the Trap Room the next day, Marsden was waiting for me. "Look what I found among the props," he said, gesturing at the table, where a checkerboard was set up. "You do know how to play, I hope."

"I like chess better," I said. "My grandfather and I used to play. I have his set back at the house."

"Unfortunately, I never learned the game."

"Okay, then—checkers. We have to keep it quiet, though. They're starting rehearsal onstage today. The set isn't finished, but Phillip wants everyone to get used to the platforms and ramps."

"Ah, yes," Marsden said, glancing up at the underside of the stage floor. "Now it begins to take shape."

As we played, I told him about Tad. About the

trick he'd tried to play with the airplane, and the burning of Pop's and Serena's pictures. Even talking about it got my heart beating hard again and choked my throat with fury. "I've been thinking about a way to get back at him."

"Sweet revenge?" Marsden said, and captured two of my checkers.

I nodded. "Phillip has arranged to have Tad and me fence this afternoon before stage combat class. Can you keep Tad from beating me?"

"Hardly sporting," he said, rubbing at his mustache. "Can't you do that on your own?"

"No way. Laurence says he's really good. But if he can't hit me, if you could deflect his foil somehow every time he comes close, it'll make him crazy. He won't know what's happening."

Marsden smiled, his eyes all twinkly. "And he'll be frightened, do you think? Just a little? If scaring him is all you're after, why do I have to do something as strenuous as fencing? Couldn't I just be ghostlike? Moan a little? Clank a few chains?"

"No. He thinks he's so good. I don't just want to keep him from beating me; I want him to look really bad. And I want him not to know why."

"So, your purpose here is to shake his confidence. Not an easy task. This would seem to be a boy of quite remarkable self-confidence."

"Arrogance, you mean."

"'Pride goeth before destruction,' says the Good Book."

"So, can you do it? Will you?"

Marsden fingered his tie and nodded. "I assume the match will be in the rehearsal room."

"Yes."

"Very well, I will do what you want."

Tad and Julia were late getting there, so Laurence and I put on our gear and fenced a while so I could get warmed up. "Your form's getting better," he said as he hit me for the third time, "but you need to work on quickness. Keep your wrist loose." I actually managed a touch, but I figured he probably let me score a point to help my confidence. When he took off his mask, he was smiling. "Don't worry— you're doing fine. Pretty soon, you'll be able to give him a real run for his money. And don't forget that sometimes knowing you're good can be something of a handicap. You get complacent."

Julia apologized when they came in—she'd been kept late at a fund-raising meeting. She settled into a chair and Tad got dressed, never looking at me. I hoped Marsden would remember to show up. And I hoped he could do what I wanted.

When we saluted each other, Tad smiled his most arrogant smile. "Hope you're ready to lose big time," he said as he put on his mask.

I felt a chill against my neck and smiled. Marsden was here. We'll see about that, I thought.

"*En garde*," Laurence said, and the match was on.

Tad lunged first, and I parried. He recovered fast

and lunged again. Before I could move to block him, his foil seemed to slide sideways in the air, and he nearly lost his balance. I tried to use the advantage to get in a hit to his open left side, but he managed to parry me and then lunged again. Again his foil slid sideways in the air, this time to his left. It's hard to see an opponent's face behind the wire mesh of his mask, but I could imagine his astonishment.

"Take it easy, Tad," Julia said. "Don't push so hard."

In the split second he took to glance her way, I got in a quick hit to his left side.

"One–zero," Laurence called.

Tad put his foil up and came at me, taking two steps as I backed away, the tip of his foil making fast little circles around mine. If he'd started this match feeling complacent, he wasn't feeling that way now. I slashed sideways against his blade. He recovered quickly and aimed a hit under my arm, directly at my heart. Again his foil angled off, just missing my jacket. "Huh?" I heard as I slid my foil in to hit him where he had nearly hit me.

"Two–zero," Laurence said, and I heard the surprise in his voice.

Tad seemed to go berserk then, and even with Marsden's help, I had to work very hard to keep from getting hit. His foil seemed to be everywhere, and he kept advancing on me, forcing me back. I parried as best I could, and the sound of foil on foil hid the fact that whenever his tip came close to hitting me, it slid harmlessly away. Then, when he was off balance from missing a particularly determined lunge, I began to move on him, forcing him to back away. Now he had to keep his attention on defending instead of attacking, but he did it well and I couldn't get close enough for a hit. He had learned what Kent had tried to drill into me, to keep his arm close to his body and use wrist action to deflect his opponent's foil rather than swinging wide and leaving himself open for a quick counterthrust.

Though I hadn't hit him, I took another step and pressed my attack, trying to get him to swing wide enough to give me an opening. Tad parried, and I had exactly the opening I wanted. As he seemed almost to pause—his chest unprotected—I felt a kind of shudder through my foil, and I lunged as hard as I could. In almost the same instant, Laurence was between us, yelling "Stop!" and slashing upward with his own foil, deflecting mine and tearing it out of my hand. It arced into the air and clattered to the floor.

The force of my lunge threw me into Laurence and Laurence into Tad and we ended up on the floor, a tangle of arms and legs. I struggled to sit up and take off my mask. "That was a clear shot!" I yelled at Laurence. "I could have hit him!"

Laurence pushed himself to his knees and then stood up, picking up his foil. He helped Tad stand and then stretched a hand to me.

I shook my head and stood on my own. "What'd you do that for?"

He pointed to my foil, lying on the floor. "Pick it up," he said. "And look at it."

I did what he said. There was a tiny dent in the bell guard where it had hit the floor, but I saw nothing else wrong with it.

"The tip."

And then I saw. The plastic tip guard was gone.

Tad tore his mask off. "You tried to kill me!"

Laurence took my foil from me, shaking his head. "The guard was on when you started. I've seen foils break and become dangerous that way, but I've never seen a tip guard come off like that. It's a good thing I noticed it was missing."

Julia picked Tad's foil up off the floor and checked its tip guard. "This is on plenty tight—"

"I checked them both earlier," Laurence said, "like I always do. They were both tight."

I remembered the shudder I'd felt in my foil just before I lunged.

Julia made a little sound in the back of her throat and went over by the window. She reached down and picked something up off the floor. The tip guard. She brought it back and Laurence took it, rolling it between his fingers, shaking his head. "It isn't cracked or broken or anything. I just don't understand."

I was pretty sure I did.

CHAPTER SIXTEEN

Julia, her face looking pale, took Tad home to shower and change. He would not be staying for stage combat class. Laurence excused me, too. I got cleaned up in the men's dressing room and went straight to the Trap Room, where I found Marsden waiting for me. He sat in the armchair, his tie loosened, his hat on his knee, grinning.

"What did you do that for?" I asked.

"You didn't want him to beat you!"

"The tip guard," I said. "You took it off. If Laurence hadn't noticed it was missing, I might have—"

"Killed the boy?" Marsden shook his head. "Not likely. You might have hurt him a bit, but the point surely wouldn't have pierced the padding of his jacket. It was different in the old days, when actors fenced in nothing but doublet and hose. An accident then would have been easy to arrange."

"I didn't say I wanted an accident."

"Ah...." Marsden fingered his watch chain for a moment and then looked up at me, his eyes oddly blank. "My mistake."

"You scared Julia."

"Perhaps. But I scared Theodore more." He chuckled. "It was a good match, I think. You did quite well, and you got what you wanted. His confidence was definitely shaken. A good trick, that. I had a splendid time!" He smiled at me, and I felt his expression was meant to tell me something I didn't quite get. "We make an excellent team, you know. Like Richard of Gloucester and Buckingham."

Before I could answer, he put on his hat and blinked out, leaving me, as always, gasping for breath and chilled to the bone. For the first time since I'd met Marsden, I had begun to feel afraid.

By the evening, though, I'd gotten over it. Marsden was right. Even without its tip guard, my foil couldn't have done much more than bruise Tad, even if I'd landed a really solid hit. The old actor was a practical joker, and he'd taken his chance to play a trick on me as well as Tad—that was all. After all, he was a ghost. How could I begrudge him a little scare now and again, even if it was at my expense? He was definitely right that my idea had worked. Tad was a mess. He barely said a word through dinner, and he didn't eat much, either—not even the strawberry shortcake Joan had fixed for dessert.

Rehearsal that night was act 1. It would be Tad's and my first rehearsal on the actual set. The lighting designer and his team were working over the dinner hour to get lighting instruments hung and generally focused so it would all feel a little more like the real thing. But when dinner was over and we were getting ready to go back to the theatre, Tad refused to go. "There's something bad there," he said. "Something dangerous."

"You are going to rehearsal," Phillip said.

"Not," Tad said.

"Tad...," Julia said, her voice carrying a warning.

"Not!" Tad repeated.

Toni jangled the van keys and the others went outside. I wanted to stay. Whatever was about to happen, I didn't want to miss it. But Toni grabbed my arm and pulled me after her through the screen door.

Outside, Kent tossed me his extra helmet. "He'll be there," he said as I climbed onto the motorcycle behind him. "I'd bet my bike on it. And on time, too."

Kent was right. Well before we were to start, Tad, his face sullen and furious, came down the center aisle between Phillip and Julia. She sat him down next to Toni in the middle of the fourth row and he didn't move until it was time for his first scene, except to glance over his shoulder every so often.

When it came time for him to go on, he moved where he was supposed to move, but with no more animation than a stick. He spoke his lines in a barely audible monotone. In our scene together, I did what I had done before, trying to make the prince as real as I could, imagining myself on the edge of having all the power in the world, threatened only by my uncle, Richard of Gloucester. But it didn't work the way it had worked before. Tad's refusal to interact pulled me down, and the energy of the scene seemed to drain away like water out of a cracked jar.

It wasn't only me—nobody seemed to be really with it this evening. Even Phillip was off.

At the end of Tad's and my scene, as the guards, played by two of the college student "warm bodies," began to lead us down the ramp that led offstage, Tad stuck his foot out and tripped me. I went down hard, skinning both knees and scraping my right elbow on the fake rock. Phillip, who was close enough to have seen exactly what happened, said nothing. I flipped Tad off as I got up, but he didn't react. He just went back to sit next to Toni again, his face frozen into a sullen mask.

During notes after the rehearsal, Phillip told me to be sure to keep my focus and energy and not let down, but he didn't say a single word to Tad.

That night, I woke up from a dream, just as it was beginning to get light. I lay there, trying to remember the dream. Something about a house. An image began to come clear: a living room with the usual living room furniture—couch, chairs, tables, television set, regular home stuff—all very comfy and expensive-looking. On the left was an open doorway leading into a theatre. It wasn't a big theatre—only about five rows of red plush seats, six seats to a row. But there was a stage, complete with curtains and lights. In the dream, that hadn't seemed strange at all.

Then I had been on the stage, with the lights full on me, wondering whether I had on the right costume, wondering what the play was and what my lines were. In a panic, I turned to the person on my left. It was Phillip. He smiled and nodded and suddenly I knew both the play and my lines. The panic went away as quickly as it had come. I turned the other way and Julia was there, smiling at me. She reached out and took my hand. A moment later, Phillip took my other hand. The audience started to applaud. The three of us had been bowing to a sea of featureless faces in an auditorium so huge, the walls were lost in the distance when I woke up.

CHAPTER SEVENTEEN

It took Tad several days to quit fighting about going to the theatre. Phillip gave him a couple of very public speeches about the responsibility of an actor always to put the good of the show before his personal comfort, the necessity of being a team player, and finally the old saying The show must go on, but none of that did any good. Marsden came up with a couple of ideas for teasing him some more, but I told him we didn't dare. I wouldn't have minded Tad getting even more scared, if that was possible, but I didn't want to hurt the show.

When we rehearsed our scene the next time, Tad started out the way he'd been before, moving like a stick, saying his lines just to say them. Phillip stopped the scene. "Listen up, Tad! Jared's never acted before in his life," he told him, "but his work is showing him to be ten times the actor you are. Unless you straighten up and get ahold of yourself, he's going to blow you right off the stage."

Tad's face went a dull red and it looked for a minute as if he was having an asthma attack or something. A deathly silence fell over the whole stage. Even the clicking of Joan's knitting needles out in the house stopped. It was as if somebody had pushed a gigantic pause button.

"Now take it from the top of the scene," Phillip said finally. Tad didn't change right in that instant. But after that, the arguments about going to the theatre stopped. You could tell he didn't want to be there. He kept glancing over his shoulder, and he jumped at any sudden noise. But at least he came, and when he had to rehearse, he rehearsed. He did stop going to stage combat class, though. Phillip couldn't very well argue with that, since neither of us had to fight in the play.

Meantime, Marsden was plenty busy being caretaker. By the end of that week, there wasn't much of anybody left who didn't believe in him—or at least wasn't too confused to argue about it. Things nobody could explain happened so often that it got impossible to pretend otherwise. Even Julia quit challenging the stories.

The technical teams seemed to be the happiest to have a helping ghost. One night when they were painting the set, a half-full can of paint got knocked off the highest platform. "It tipped as it fell," the girl who'd knocked it off told everybody the next day, "but then it just suddenly righted itself, like somebody had caught it in midair. After that, it fell so slowly that when it landed on the next level down— right side up—the paint didn't even splash out. I'm telling you, I saw it!"

The guy whose shoelaces I'd tied together had been painting that night, too, and he agreed that that was exactly what had happened.

After that, they figured every other minute the ghost was doing something to help out. Some of the things they thought Marsden did, he told me he didn't have anything to do with. People forgot where they put a tool and then found it suddenly and were sure the ghost had put it there. Once while the lighting designer was hanging a light instrument, he leaned too far out from the ladder and almost fell. He managed to catch hold of the light pipe and get himself balanced again, but he was convinced that he and the light would both have gone crashing to the seats beneath if it hadn't been for the ghost.

"If I *had* been there, I would have let the light fall, so I could catch it at the last minute and astound the assembled watchers," Marsden said later.

Sometimes, with the actors, he played tricks. He took something from where they had put it and made it turn up somewhere else, just when they were starting to go nuts looking for it. Several times, Joan found her knitting on a seat in the theatre when she had left it in the dressing room. But instead of getting upset, she decided that the ghost was looking after her, so she began leaving it on purpose so that Marsden would bring it to her. Once, she said she saw him doing it. Her description of him sounded right—she mentioned his mustache and his hat—but she also said she could see through him. I couldn't decide whether she wasn't all that good at seeing him or whether he hadn't made the effort to fully materialize.

Aside from Tad, who thought the ghost was out to get him, George was the only one who refused to be convinced that the ghost was either friendly or a sign of good luck. Since I wouldn't let Marsden tease Tad, he focused his mischievous side on George. He hid the crosswords so often, George quit doing them. When he wasn't onstage, George would either sit in the theatre with his arms crossed and a look of martyrdom on his face or leave the building altogether. He saw Marsden a few times, too, and from the way he described what he'd seen—the evil sneer, the nasty laugh—I decided the old actor was doing his best to scare George. Marsden *had* played Richard, after all—he wouldn't have any trouble appearing to be a villain.

As it got closer to opening night, the stage began to look more and more like a bleak, rocky planet. The padded, glue-hardened fabric on the set walls was painted a dull yellow-brown color first, which had just made it look like yellow-brown glue-hardened fabric. But then the paint crew went to work with other colors, brushing and spraying and spattering so that it looked more and more like rock. You had to get up really close to see that it wasn't real. Lights were set at intervals into the walls, covered with a gauzy fabric painted like the rest of the set, so that when the lights weren't turned on, you couldn't see them. That way, the set could seem to be the daylight surface of the planet in one scene and tunnels in the next, when the stage lights were dimmed and the wall lights came on.

The black curtains at the back of the stage had been taken down and some kind of stretchy fabric put in their place, pulled tight behind the set so that when the lights on it changed, it looked like the sky. It could go from dark night, with pinpricks of stars, to dawn, pink at the bottom changing to blue at the top, to the full blue of daylight, to dusk.

The trapdoors must have been great for making theatre magic when Marsden was alive, but the magic the tech people could create now, with a computer running the lights and high-tech sound speakers, was really impressive.

"Listen up, ghosts!" Phillip said one night after rehearsal. "We'll need you for filming first thing tomorrow morning—full makeup and costumes." I'd been wondering why we had never blocked the ghost scene, and now Phillip explained. The ghost speeches were all going to be filmed. Then, during the performance, the film would be projected onto a background of fog made by a fog machine. That way, the ghosts would be translucent images, moving against the swirling fog. The voices would come from speakers both at the front of the house and at the back, with just enough reverberation added to make them sound ghostly.

Everybody thought it was a great idea. So did I. Not authentic, maybe, for somebody who knew what a ghost looked like, but a great idea.

CHAPTER EIGHTEEN

Tad and I hadn't seen much of each other that week. I was still doing my best to be in our room only when he was either sound asleep or not there. But the next morning, we didn't have a choice. We were in the little dressing room together, getting into our ghost costumes. The dressing room was small and cramped to begin with, but now the black curtains that had been taken down from the stage had been hung on a rack against the wall and our costumes were on a smaller rack just inside the door, so there wasn't all that much room left for us.

The room, with its new bright lights, was still a little chilly and damp, but the counters and mirrors had been cleaned and our chairs set in place. It wasn't quite as nasty in there as it had been. Toni had brought us a couple of vanilla room deodorizers, so it didn't smell as bad either. Tad's makeup box—a big three-tiered tackle box with his name on it—was open in front of the mirror where I'd first seen the face. But I couldn't see anything there now except the streaks and smudges of the old silvering.

Even with the lights and deodorizers, I wasn't crazy about having the door closed, but we needed to change. Tad took off his shorts and T-shirt and dropped them on the floor. Wearing only his underpants, he sat down at his place and began rooting through his makeup kit.

At my place was a cigar box with some makeup that Toni had scrounged for me. But I didn't know what to do with it. I thought maybe I'd just watch Tad and copy what he did. I certainly wasn't going to ask for his help! I took off my own shorts and shirt, folded them carefully, and put them on the counter. Pop would never believe how neat I'd made myself become, just to show I wasn't a slob like Tad. I took my costume down from the rack and started to put it on.

"What are you doing?" Tad asked.

"What does it look like I'm doing? I'm putting my costume on."

"Don't you know anything? You have to put on your makeup before your costume. You want to get makeup all over it?"

I hung it back up and sat down, doing my best to watch Tad without being obvious about it. When he pulled a sponge out of his kit, I saw a crumpled pack of cigarettes in the bottom compartment—the same brand Toni smoked. He'd only had one cigarette before, and now he had a whole pack. He must be smoking fairly regularly. No wonder he chewed gum all the time. I figured he must have stolen the pack from Toni. Since she was supposed to have quit, she wasn't likely to report any missing.

Julia came in just then and Tad hurriedly pulled a pack of tissues over the cigarettes to hide them. My face and ears got hot with embarrassment to be sitting there in my underpants, but Julia didn't even seem to notice.

"I thought you might need some help with your makeup," she said to me. "All you really need is clown white."

"He stole mine," Tad said.

"I did not!"

Julia pointed to the tube in front of Tad. "Then what's that?"

"I found it and took it back."

She sighed, dug a tube and sponge out of my box, and began smoothing the white makeup onto my cheeks. "The idea is to cover the skin completely, face, neck, ears, and hands, making it as smooth as you can. I'll come back later and do your eyeliner and spray your hair."

"I need help doing the back of my neck," Tad said.

"You can help each other. I have my own to do."

"I'm not helping him. He—"

Julia threw the sponge down on the counter. "Stop it! Just stop it! This is making me crazy! I have enough to worry about: Can we raise enough money to get through the season? Will anybody come? Will anybody like it?" Her voice rose, getting shriller and shriller. "I can't worry about whether the two of you can stand each other! If you don't figure out a way to get along with each other, I'm going to go stark staring mad! Do you hear me? Stark staring mad!" She flung the tube of white makeup against the mirror and stormed out.

I just sat there, staring at the sponge on the counter and the smudge of white it had made when it hit. Where had that come from? In the mirror, Tad looked as astonished as I felt. The room felt danker suddenly, and I noticed the smell more than I had. Maybe it was the room that had gotten to her.

When she came back later to do our eyes and hair, she didn't speak to either of us any more than she had to. She just finished very fast, and left.

Our regular costumes were coveralls like the ones the guards and soldiers wore, but more elaborate, with extra piping and pockets and belts, and the royal crest on the breast pocket. Tad's was blue and gold and mine was red and gold, with an extra row of piping along the seams to show that I was the crown prince. The ghost costumes were exactly the same, except all white.

When we were both dressed, we were totally white, our faces and hands and even our hair, which had been sprayed with white hair spray—totally white except for a heavy line of black around our eyes and gray smudges under our eyes and cheekbones that made us look more sick, I thought, than dead. I hoped Marsden was hanging around somewhere close by. He'd get a kick out of what ghosts were supposed to look like.

It was a strange, stark-white group of actors that gathered on the stage. George, on the middle platform with a movie camera on a tripod, was getting ready to do the filming. "We're going to integrate music with the lines," Phillip said, "so watch carefully for my signal once you get into place and the filming begins. You'll hear the music through the speakers, so you'll get a sense of the rhythm of it, but I'll cue you. Think of me as a conductor. We can do as many takes as we need, but obviously the sooner we get this done, the sooner you'll be able to get cleaned up and get that stuff out of your hair. Tad and Jared, I know you haven't had any rehearsal on this, but I want the unison to be as exact as you can make it. When it's your turn, we'll try it a few times before we start the camera rolling so you can work on timing and rhythm." I nodded. "Tad?" Tad shrugged and nodded, too.

"Okay, let's get going. You set, George?"

George fiddled with his camera for a moment and then nodded.

"Okay. Remember, everyone, each of you is cursing Richard. Like everybody else in his world, he *believes* in curses! So make them good. Ferocious! This is the man who murdered you and this is your chance for revenge. Tomorrow is the decisive battle. Richard has more men; he's likely to win. You mean to see that he doesn't."

I sat in the front row to watch the filming. One by one, the ghosts of the people Richard had murdered prophesied that he would remember what he had done to them as he faced his enemy in battle the next day. All their curses ended with the same words: "despair, and die!" Even watching them in real life, just actors with white makeup on, the combination of music and their words was powerful. I could imagine what it would be like in the play, with their images projected on the swirling fog.

Finally, it was Tad's and my turn. We went to stand on the platform, and Phillip had the sound technician play our music through once so we could get a feel for it. Then he had us practice. The first couple of times, he wasn't satisfied. Tad kept getting ahead of me, as if we were racing to see who could finish first.

He told Tad to slow down, and as we were about to begin again, I felt a chill along the back of my neck. I glanced around and saw nothing. Then, off to my right, beyond the edge of the platform where we were standing, it seemed to me I caught a glimpse of movement, a kind of blur in the air. So Marsden *had* come to watch. George, too, seemed to sense something. He shuddered suddenly and looked over his shoulder, first to one side, then the other. After a moment, he shrugged.

"Let's take it from the beginning again," Phillip said. "Stand closer together!" Tad didn't move, so I stepped closer to him, until our shoulders were touching. "Good. Now listen to each other and stay together!" That time, we did better. As Phillip was telling us what he'd liked about that version, I saw George suddenly frown and squint at the place where I was pretty sure Marsden was watching. A second after that, I felt Tad shiver, the movement noticeable all the way down his arm. He, too, was looking at the air at the end of the platform. Did he see something? There was nothing more than a hint of that blur in the air.

"Tad, remember to say your lines directly into the camera!" Phillip didn't seem to have noticed anything. "Okay, you two, I think you're ready. Make it real." Tad was still staring. "Tad! Now remember, this is the man who ordered you to be smothered in your beds. Camera!" George, still frowning, gave him a thumbs-up. "Music!" The music began, building and then fading as he cued us.

"Dream on thy cousins smothered in the Tower. Let us be lead within thy bosom, Richard, and weigh thee down to ruin, shame, and death! Thy nephews' souls bid thee"—Phillip held his hand up to indicate the pause, the music swelled, and he cued us to raise our voices over the music—"despair, and die!"

"Good. Great! Let's just do it one more time to be sure we have it!"

Tad and George were both looking toward

Marsden again. "I think we got it," George said. "Can we just move on to Lady Anne?" He cleared his throat. "Just two more—let's get this done and get out of here. We have company."

"Company?" Phillip turned to look at George. "What—" He looked where George was pointing.

Now I could almost make out Marsden's outline, like an unfocused space, distorting the edges of the objects behind it. Tad's hands were shaking and he shoved them into his pockets.

"All right, we'll move on." Phillip waved us away. "You're dismissed for now. Don't change yet, though. If"—he glanced at George—"if anything changes, we may want to do another take."

Tad left, taking the platform steps two at a time, and headed for the dressing room as if Marsden were chasing him. As I sat down in the house to watch the rest of the filming, it was all I could do not to laugh out loud.

CHAPTER NINETEEN

By the time Julia's part had been filmed, Marsden was gone. I knew because I had felt him brush past me on his way up the aisle. When they started on Buckingham's curse—the last one—George had relaxed. He told Del not to worry, there was plenty of film and they could do as many takes as they needed.

"In that case," Phillip said, "let's do the princes again just to make sure. We won't know what we have till the film's processed, and I don't want to have to do this all over again."

"No problem," George said.

"Ghosts, stay in costume till you're dismissed," Toni called. Then she told me to go get Tad. "We'll do your bit again in about ten minutes."

Ten minutes would be plenty of time to find out

how Marsden had liked the ghosts. Tad had closed the dressing room door again, so I didn't bother to go in. I knocked, and there was a scuffling sound inside. "Who's there?" he said. "Don't come in; I'm not dressed."

"Big deal," I said. "It's just me. You aren't supposed to be out of costume anyway. They want us to do our scene again in about ten minutes."

Tad didn't answer.

"The ghost's gone. There's nothing to be afraid of," I added.

"Who says I'm afraid?"

I do, I thought, as I headed down to the Trap Room. Marsden wasn't there. I called to him a couple of times and he didn't appear, so I sat down to wait. After a while, I got the old familiar sensation, and I was still gasping for breath when Marsden popped into full view, sitting on the arm of the chair. No matter how many times he did it, it still gave me the willies in the worst way. I could understand the way George felt, if this was what it was like for him every time Marsden was around, whether he could be seen or not.

"Disappointing, really," Marsden said, tweaking his mustache. "I've seen much better ghosts on the stage. You should have seen the apparition of Hamlet's father in the production at the Theatre Royal...."

"You haven't really seen these ghosts yet," I told him. "Wait'll the film's developed and you see them projected onto fog."

Marsden began telling me about the ghost of Hamlet's father then, but his heart didn't seem to be in it. He kept pausing and looking off over my head as if he was thinking about something else. Finally, he said he felt a call for the ghostly caretaker. Ten seconds later, he was gone, and I was shivering and gasping and thinking how much easier it would be to be friends with a regular, live human being. I went on back to the theatre, wondering what Marsden had gone off to do.

Onstage, Del was still cursing Richard. He must have goofed a couple times, I thought, to be taking so long. Tad wasn't there yet. I figured they'd probably make me go get him when they were ready for us. Just what I wanted to be, Tad's personal messenger. Toni caught my eye and held up one hand to show me it would be about five minutes yet before we'd have to do our scene. I nodded and sat down. Let Toni go get him if he wasn't here by then.

The music began its swell behind Buckingham's voice. "O, in the battle think on Buckingham, and die in terror of thy guiltiness! Dream on, dream on, of bloody deeds and death—" Del coughed. "I'm sorry. Can we take it again?"

George muttered a curse of his own and then nodded. "The miracle of film editing—just take it from 'Dream on....'"

Suddenly, the side curtains on stage left billowed up and the temperature dropped, as if an icy wind were blowing from the dressing room area toward the stage. "What the...," Del said as the curtains grazed the edge of the platform he was standing on. Before anyone could say or do anything, a thunderous pounding began on the stage-center platform. I looked toward the sound and Marsden blinked into sight, his hat askew, stamping his feet and pointing offstage. "Fire!" he shouted, his voice filling the whole theatre as if he were shouting into a bullhorn. "Fire!"

Could anybody else see and hear him? In her place in the fourth row, Toni, her hands over her ears, was looking wildly from one side of the stage to the other, trying to locate the source of the pounding. On the front of the stage, Phillip was staring directly at Marsden but doing nothing, his face a mask of confusion. But George, moving so fast that he knocked over the tripod and movie camera, vaulted off the platform and plunged through the still-moving curtains. He must be the only one who can hear Marsden's voice, I thought as the other actors, some of them looking toward Marsden, some shaking their heads in confusion, began coming down the aisles from where they had been sitting, heading toward the stage.

"Bring another fire extinguisher!" George's voice boomed over the sound of Marsden's stomping. "Hurry!"

"Fire!" Julia yelled then. "There's a fire!" And everyone began, finally, to move with some purpose and sense. Phillip ran offstage right. An earsplitting alarm began to ring, drowning out all other sound.

Phillip came back with a fire extinguisher in his hands and followed the others, who had headed off left after George.

I found myself standing onstage, in front of the platform, though I didn't remember coming up out of the house. I looked up at Marsden, who had stopped stamping when the alarm began. He straightened his hat, grinned, and winked. "Never fear," he said, his voice somehow clear over the alarm. "The theatre ghost has saved the day!"

"You didn't set a fire!"

He shook his head. "No, I didn't. Tad did. I rather suspect they will have rescued him by now." He winked again. "Pity."

I looked into his eyes, trying to tell whether he was joking or not. Of course he was, I told myself, shoving my suddenly cold hands into the pockets of my costume to warm them.

The next little while was all a confusion of fire trucks arriving, firemen in full gear fanning out through the theatre, searching every crack and crevice for hidden sparks or flames. They'd been told the moment they arrived that it had been nothing but a trash-can fire, confined to the small dressing room and put out with fire extinguishers before it did any major damage, but they didn't seem to believe it. Or maybe they felt they needed to do something to justify all the equipment they'd brought. An emergency vehicle had come, too, shortly after the fire trucks, and the medics checked

Tad for smoke inhalation and gave him oxygen for a few minutes before they left.

When all the trucks had finally gone, Phillip called the company together in the theatre. Everyone was there except for Julia and Tad. He explained that a fire "of uncertain origin" had started in the trash can in the small dressing room and that Tad had tried to put it out but that it had gotten too big too fast. In the smoke and confusion, he had become disoriented and gotten himself badly tangled in the back curtains. The rack they were hanging on had fallen on him, so he hadn't been able to get away. He had been terribly frightened, but he hadn't been really hurt. "He's shaken, but he'll be all right."

"He's lucky the ghost warned us," Toni said. She turned to George. "That ought to be enough to convince even you! The ghost saved Tad's life!"

"Maybe all of our lives!" Joan added.

"And the theatre," Del said.

George ran a hand through his thinning hair and nodded. "All right, all right. I concede. I saw him and I heard him, and I concede. He warned us about the fire. At the very least, he saved Tad's life." He grimaced. "But you still can't make me like him!"

And then everyone was talking at once. As I'd thought, George and I were the only ones who had heard Marsden's voice, but everyone who'd been there had seen the curtains, and everyone—even people who'd been in other parts of the building— had heard the stomping. Several people claimed to have seen him. They all mentioned his hat and mustache, but there was no way to know whether they'd gotten that idea from Joan's earlier description or whether they'd seen him that clearly themselves. All those who'd seen him agreed, though, that he'd been pointing offstage toward the dressing room as he stamped his feet.

"Take an extra half hour for lunch," Phillip said then. "Afternoon rehearsal will be as announced. We'll take a chance that we have enough good footage to do a decent edit of the ghost scenes; if not, we'll just have to try again early in the week. Whoever is called this afternoon, be back here at one-thirty sharp." Then he turned to me. "Jared, I'd like a word with you before you go to lunch."

I nodded. I didn't like the way he'd said my name. Phillip stood, leaning against the stage, as the others gathered their things and went off, the ghosts to the dressing rooms to change, the others to get lunch. I could feel my hands getting damp with sweat. What was the matter?

When everyone had left, Phillip crossed his arms and gave a huge sigh. He looked at me, his eyebrows nearly meeting in a deep frown. "Tad told us," he said.

"Told you what?"

"How the fire started. It charred the counter and the chairs and broke a mirror and melted a lot of makeup, but most of the damage was on Tad's side, where the trash can was. There's no point denying it.

The cigarettes were still there in your makeup box."

"In *my* box? I've never smoked a cigarette in my life!"

Phillip shook his head and sighed again. "The cigarettes were there, Jared. Julia saw them when Tad was still hysterical from being nearly smothered by the smoke and curtains. She says they weren't there when she helped you with your makeup."

I remembered the scuffling sound when I'd knocked at the dressing room door. Tad hadn't known it was me. He must have hidden the cigarettes in my box right then. He must have dropped his cigarette into the trash can then, too.

"There's no point in lying about it," Phillip said.

"It isn't a lie."

Phillip went on as if I hadn't spoken. "Apparently, your cigarette butt wasn't completely out when you threw it away. It must have smoldered quite a while before it actually started the fire. You endangered not only Tad's life but the theatre and everyone in the company, Jared. I know it was an accident, but it wouldn't have happened if you hadn't been smoking in the first place."

I almost told him Tad had stolen those cigarettes from Toni, but even if she admitted she'd been smoking, and I wasn't sure she would, the very fact that I knew her secret made it look as if I was the one who'd taken them. Especially if Tad claimed he didn't know. And Tad didn't have the slightest trouble lying.

"I know it hasn't been easy on you, Jared, but it hasn't been easy on any of us, suddenly having to... blend a family like this. I want you to be on your best behavior from now on. There is to be no more smoking."

I started to protest, but he raised his hand to stop me.

"And I want you to do everything you can to get along better with Tad. He says you've been hostile to him from the beginning. I don't expect the two of you to behave like brothers. But I *do* expect you to treat each other decently."

I nodded.

"Then that's that. I hope that, with a little more time, we can make this work. That we won't have to make different arrangements until your grandfather recovers. Do you think we can?" I nodded again. "All right. Go get out of your costume and makeup and go to lunch. You'll be using the bigger men's dressing room until we get Tad's and yours cleaned up."

I got up then and sidled out of the row of seats, feeling numb. "I don't expect the two of you to behave like brothers," Phillip had said. How did brothers behave? Richard had killed his.

Chapter Twenty

It didn't take any time at all for the word to get around the company that I had started the fire. Toni was really upset. "I *thought* there was a pack missing out of my carton," she said. "That's what I get for sharing my secret. Don't you dare ever set foot in my room again!" I'd never been in her room, of course, but I didn't bother to deny it. Everybody else believed Tad—why shouldn't she? It wasn't as if I could prove it. People seemed to look at me differently after that.

But the change in Tad was worse. The ghost had saved his life. It was the main topic of conversation at dinner, everybody congratulating him, as if he was some kind of hero. You'd think it was *Tad* who had saved the theatre, instead of the ghost. Nobody even laughed at his ridiculous story that the curtains had leapt out at him and tangled him up. They probably just thought it proved how much of a shock the fire had been to him. The fire *I'd* been careless enough to cause, of course, and he'd been doing his best to put out.

I could practically see his head swelling as people talked about it. In a flash, he'd gone from terrified to invincible. And the ghost had gone from his enemy to his ally—a kind of personal bodyguard.

I was scheduled to clear the table after dinner and he was supposed to dry the pots and pans. But he'd been excused from work detail because of his "trauma." Still, when everybody else left the dining room, he stayed on, Hamlet curled at his feet. "The ghost's on my side," he gloated as I stacked plates. "So you better watch how you treat me from now on. He's taking care of me."

"I wouldn't be too sure. Hamlet doesn't like him," I reminded him. Hamlet, hearing his name, thumped his tail on the floor. "Maybe he knows something you don't."

"Hamlet's a dog," Tad said. "What does he know?" Then, looking me right in the eye, he turned his glass upside down, so the milk he hadn't finished poured over the table and down onto his chair and the floor. Hamlet pushed himself to his feet and began lapping it up. "Oh, just look at that mess!" he said, and walked out.

When I went to our room that night after staying in the living room for the late movie, which I'd had to force myself to stay awake for, I found my futon sopping wet. Tad, who was either sleeping or doing a good job of pretending, must have poured about a gallon of water on it. I had actually started out the door to go tell Phillip and Julia when I imagined, suddenly, how he'd play the scene. "I told Jared it was an accident," he would say, blinking his eyes in perfect innocence, "and I was sorry. It was only an accident—just like when he nearly burned down the theatre."

I managed to get the mattress draped over the closet door to dry, threw my sheets into the laundry hamper, and then took my pillow outside and slept on the backseat of the van.

"He'll be unstoppable now!" I told Marsden the next day. "My life is over. You should never have done it!"

He looked up at me from under his hat brim and smiled a maddening smile. "What would you have had me do? Let him burn to death? Let the opera house—*my* opera house—burn to the ground?"

He had me there. "Well, no..."

"I did my best to frighten him," he said, examining the fingernails of one hand. "I put the light out and tangled him in the curtains. He was so terrified, he pulled the whole rack over on himself." He buffed his nails on the lapel of his coat and examined them again. "After that, I had no choice but to get him help. You can hardly blame me for the fact that his relief at being rescued turns out to be stronger than his fear of ghosts."

I sank onto the hassock. Marsden was right, of course. "Phillip says I'm to be on my best behavior."

I sighed and repeated what I had said before. "He'll be unstoppable!"

"We'll think of something," Marsden said.

Tad's little pranks went on. He dumped all my boxes out onto the floor of our room, and when I got everything put away again, he dumped all the drawers in my dresser. He tore the pages out of two paperback books. I began taking the things that were most important to me to the theatre a few at a time and stashing them in the Trap Room, where he couldn't get at them. So then he squeezed out all my toothpaste and poured my shampoo down the drain. Kent's extra helmet disappeared from his motorcycle in the theatre parking lot, so I couldn't ride with him anymore. At least Kent didn't blame me; he figured it had been stolen.

Through it all, I kept quiet. I kept remembering what Phillip had said—about making other arrangements. Having found out how I really felt about the theatre, the prospect of losing it was too terrible to think about. I spent most of the days when I wasn't called for rehearsal hiding out in the Trap Room, staying out of everybody's way. I read, I listened to tapes on Pop's old boom box, I played solitaire, and, when Marsden appeared, we played checkers and I listened to his stories of life on the road. My time with Marsden was the only good time except for when I got to be onstage.

Meanwhile, the set went on changing. The

Tower, which looked something like a gigantic termite mound, open at the top, was my favorite piece of it. The part facing the audience wasn't regular cloth like the rest of the set; it was made of scrim, a material something like black window screen that you could see through. It was painted to look like rock, just like all the rest, and when the lights were shining on it from the front, that's how it looked—like the rest of the set. But when lights came up behind the scrim, you could see right through it. The rock disappeared and you saw the two-level platform behind—the Tower room.

The real props and costumes began to appear, too. Sewing machines hummed steadily in the costume shop, where three more women and a couple of college kids had joined Phyllis. During rehearsals, guards and soldiers began wearing sleek futuristic helmets and carrying the part laser gun, part sword weapons. They had hand grips and triggers but could be used more like sabers in close-up fighting. They made a zapping sound when the trigger was pulled.

When the opening was a week away, rehearsals became run-throughs, where whole acts, and sometimes two in a row, were run from beginning to end without stopping. If someone goofed, they just had to go on, figuring out how to get past the goof, the way they would have to if there was an audience.

When Phillip called a run-through of act 4, though, he remembered that we hadn't actually set the scene where the princes are murdered in their beds in the Tower. We all knew how it was to go. Tad and I were to be lying in bed on the high platform of the Tower and Kent, as Tyrrel, the murderer, was to sneak up from the lower platform as sinister music played and smother us in our sleep. But we'd never actually done the scene because there weren't any lines to memorize and the bed and pillows and covers hadn't been ready. Now the props were all there, so on Friday afternoon, we were called to block it.

"At this point," Phillip said as we started, "all the distinctions between the two princes are lost. There's no more question of which one is next in the line of succession—they're just two more stumbling blocks in Richard's way and they're about to be snuffed out. So we won't actually see either of you, except as bodies in the bed. You'll be lying under just the sheet, with the comforter tangled up at your feet. Kent, you'll stand looking at them for a moment and then you'll pull the comforter up as if you're about to cover them. You know, like a mother tucking them in. Except that when you pull it up, you'll hold it down over the face of the first one. He'll kick and struggle a little—not enough to wake his brother—and when he stops moving, you'll do the same to the other. Then you'll stand for a moment, making sure they're dead, before you creep away. The music will continue and the lights will stay up for a count of, say, ten, maybe fifteen. We want to give the audience plenty of time to get it. And then lights and music out and lights up on me, down below, as you come to give me the news. So let's try it."

The bed was nothing like a real bed. It was just a small, narrow platform, built on an angle so that our heads would be about a foot higher than our feet. That was to let the audience see us even though we were pretty far above them. A foam cushion had been stapled to the wood to make it comfortable, and a low footboard ran across the bottom to keep us from sliding off. The pillows were stapled in place, too, so they wouldn't slip. A sheet was draped over the bed and another sheet and a dark gray comforter lay across the foot.

"Who goes where?" Tad asked.

"Doesn't matter," Phillip said. "How about you stage left, and Jared stage right."

I got onto the bed and Tad followed. It was so narrow, we were practically on top of each other. Kent covered us with the sheet and Tad jabbed me a couple of times with his elbow. I didn't react.

"All right. Get into a sleeping position." We turned on our sides, our backs to each other. "No, curl together—like spoons. Good. You both okay?"

"Okay," I said.

Tad jabbed me again. "Okay."

"So let's try it. No moving now, Tad. You're asleep."

I lay there, feeling the heat of Tad's body against me. I heard Kent's footsteps as he moved up from the lower platform. Then I felt him pull the comforter up over us.

"Which one first?" he asked.

"Stage left," Phillip said. "You'd do the closer one first so you wouldn't have to lean over a sleeping kid and risk waking him up—and Jared, when he gets to you, go ahead and put up a real fight before you die."

I felt Kent's hand push down between my head and Tad's. Tad began kicking and struggling. His feet and his fists hit me and his elbows jabbed into my stomach.

"Not so hard," Phillip called to him. "I don't want it to look as if your brother would wake up. And no sounds! The only thing we should hear is the music."

Tad didn't stop struggling, and he didn't stop hollering. "No, no, no!" His voice was muffled by the comforter but plenty loud enough to hear.

"Tad, stop!" Phillip called. "You have to stop before Kent can let up on you. He has to think you're dead."

Instantly, Tad stopped struggling. Almost before Kent moved, Tad had torn the comforter off and sat up. He was crying. "No!" he screamed. "I can't, I can't! I can't do this!"

"Of course you can," Phillip said as Tad climbed out of the bed and stood at the front of the platform, shaking, tears streaming down his red face. "It'll only last a few seconds. The moment you stop struggling, he'll let up and do Jared."

"It's like in the fire. It's like the curtains on me in the fire! I feel like I'm smothering! I can't do it!"

Phillip sighed. "All right, then, switch places. You *can* stand the sheet over your face—"

Tad scrubbed at his tears with both hands, then nodded.

"Fine. Switch places and Kent can smother Jared first."

"I'll only bring the comforter up over your chin," Kent told him. "Just enough to make it look right from the audience."

Tad gulped and swallowed. "Leave it like that, then. Make sure you don't leave it over my face when you go!"

"Okay."

And so we changed places and Kent tried again. Again, Tad started crying and struggling the minute Kent got the comforter near his face. We tried it different ways, until Phillip finally lost his temper. "Tad, get ahold of yourself. Nothing bad is happening to you! After a few seconds of struggling, you have to go limp."

"I can't help it!"

"Of course you can. Just do it. Kent isn't putting it over your face, so you just have to *lie still*. Absolutely still! The audience has to believe the princes are both dead. You're a professional—start acting like it!"

And—again—it worked. Tad was determined to prove he was a pro. I wasn't. He was.

It wasn't till later, till I told Marsden about it, that the idea for getting back at Tad came up. I don't even remember who thought of it—me or Marsden.

CHAPTER TWENTY-ONE

That night, my futon was soaked again. This time, Tad didn't pretend to be asleep. He just lay there, one arm around Hamlet's neck, grinning at me as I took my pillow and headed back downstairs. I'd been chewed alive by mosquitoes the night I spent in the van. So this time, I decided to sleep on the couch in the living room. That meant waiting till everybody else had gone off to bed. It also meant sleeping on lumps and sags and what felt like a two-by-four down the middle of my back.

By the time everybody gathered for breakfast, I had showered, gotten dressed, and polished off the last two bowls of Tad's Cocoa Puffs.

Later that morning, while Phillip ran individual scenes in the theatre overhead, Marsden and I played checkers. I told him about Tad's reaction to the smothering scene.

"He said it reminded him of the fire and being tangled in the curtains."

"I told you I'd frightened him," he said.

And suddenly, whoever it was that thought of it first, there was the idea. It was simple enough. I could tell Kent I had a message from Phillip that he'd changed his mind about the smothering scene. He wanted Kent to walk around the bed, looking at the sleeping princes, thinking about how to do what he was supposed to do, and then play the whole scene from the other side. I could tell him that Tad and I were going to change places so that he'd still be smothering me first.

Only I wouldn't tell Tad and we wouldn't change places. So when Kent went to smother me, it would really be Tad. It would be Tad who'd have the comforter over his whole face afterward—over his mouth and nose. Tad would have to be the professional actor and hold totally still the whole time Kent pretended to smother me, totally still while the music played and the lights stayed on to give the audience time to understand that the princes were dead.

"Opening night is when you must do it," Marsden said, jumping the checker I'd decided to sacrifice. "With an audience, he won't be able to do anything but lie there."

I grinned. "Yeah. He's too much of a pro to wreck

opening night. He'll go nuts. Completely nuts!"

And that was that. No big deal, just a way to get back at Tad for everything he'd done to me. For the futon, the cigarettes—everything.

Marsden won that checker game. But it wasn't a fair competition. I hadn't been concentrating. "I'll get you back later," I promised as he gloated. "But not this afternoon. It's tech run-through and I'm going to stay for the whole thing." All the set pieces and all the actual props were going to be used, and the lighting and sound crews would be working out all their cues. I wanted to be there to see how it all came together.

Marsden said we could play checkers as often as I liked, but he would always win. Then, twisting his mustache ends dramatically, he smiled and blinked out. When I was breathing normally again, I looked up at the underside of the stage, where the sounds of heavy feet told me they were working the final fight scene. I realized suddenly that I cared about that— the stage over my head and the play we were doing—as much as, maybe more than, I'd cared about anything else in my whole life. That—and an old actor who'd been dead more than a hundred years and who still nearly scared the pants off me every time he came and went.

It was Saturday, and the show was to open June twenty-ninth, the following Thursday. The pace of everything had sped up. Tech people were every-where, like ants in an ant colony, suddenly serious and concentrated instead of goofing around. And most of the actors had gotten testy. Even Joan quit smiling and humming and knitting long enough to throw a temper tantrum about her costume.

The last couple of run-throughs had taken a little over two hours, but that afternoon running just the first three acts took clear till dinnertime. Everything had to stop and start and stop again while sound cues or light cues got rewritten and tried different ways. There was a fair amount of cursing and a lot of complaining, mostly from the actors. Watching it all was boring sometimes, but it was fun, too, to see the technical stuff start to work.

Acts four and five were to be run after dinner, so I told Marsden to be sure and be there. This would be the first time they'd do the ghost scene for real, with the film and the fog instead of Toni reading the ghosts' lines. Plus, they'd be adding all the *Star Wars* light and sound magic to the fight scenes at the end. I wanted him to see it all.

In the scene in act 4 where Tad and I got smothered, Kent didn't really do the whole bit with the comforter; he just sort of made the motions. So Tad spent half the scene jabbing his elbows into my stomach again. The lights and music didn't time out together exactly right the first time through, so we had to do it again.

Just before we started the second time, I felt Marsden come in. He tugged at the sheet by my feet, and when I sat up, I could see that sort of glimmer in the air moving across the stage. I wasn't the only one who noticed.

"I think we've got company again," Phillip said.

Toni was up in the booth now, hooked into the system with headphones, instead of out in the house. "What?" she asked, her voice coming over the speakers.

"Nothing. Just the ghost!" Phillip said. "He's come to watch."

"Tell him we need all the help we can get!"

Tad sat up and peered into the dark house. "Where is he?"

"If the two of you are such good buddies, how come you can't see him?" I said.

"All right, all right, let's go on," Phillip said. "With or without supernatural help, we've got miles to go before we sleep."

During the rest of the rehearsal, Marsden moved from one part of the theatre to another, sometimes sitting in the house, sometimes going onto the stage. I couldn't always tell where he was, but several times people reacted when he came close. And once, when a light turned out to be focused too far downstage to pick up the actor it was supposed to, before the cursing tech kid could start up to the attic to refocus it, the light moved all by itself until it was shining exactly where it was needed. "Thanks," the kid called up to it, shaking his head.

The first time they did the ghost scene, the fog machine hadn't put out enough fog by the time the projector came on, so the ghosts were more voice than image. But when they tried it again, using more fog juice, it worked perfectly. If I hadn't spent the last few weeks hanging out with a real ghost, playing checkers with him, watching him fiddle with his hat and try to make his watch work, I'd have believed in these ghosts. As the fog swirled and moved, the translucent images swirled and moved, floating over Richard's bed like the disembodied spirits ghosts were supposed to be. The voices reverberated through the theatre, woven into the music, so that it was hard to sort out which was which.

"Fainting, despair; despairing, yield thy breath!" the ghost of Buckingham said, and the last echoes died as Phillip sat up, clutching at his chest.

"Soft! I did but dream. O coward conscience, how dost thou afflict me!"

In the dark house, I shivered and gasped as Marsden appeared in the seat next to me. He leaned close and whispered in my ear, "All right, I admit it. They're better than Hamlet's father." And he blinked out again, leaving me choking, halfway between a gasp and a laugh.

CHAPTER
TWENTY-TWO

I didn't see much of Marsden over the next couple of days. Sunday was the actors' day off, and since I didn't have anything to do, I volunteered to work tech. The actors were off, but the tech people were working harder than ever. I'd thought the set was done—it looked pretty good to me—but it hadn't been fully "dressed," which meant that there were lots of little details that hadn't been added yet. The lighting designer wanted a bunch of the color gels on the lights changed and there was a glitch that had to be fixed in the computer that ran the light board. The costume people seemed the most frantic, because Monday was the first dress rehearsal and lots of costumes weren't finished yet. I spent most of the day making papier-mâché rocks to strew around the edges of the set once the stage floor was painted and hot-gluing Richard's boar's head insignia onto the helmets of his soldiers and fleurs-de-lis on the helmets of the enemy. I never got down to the Trap Room at all.

On Monday, things were every bit as frantic, only now the actors were there, too, and the big question was who got to be onstage when—actors or techies. The actors had union rules that said they could only rehearse for seven hours, so Phillip took two hours in the morning for the first three acts, two hours in the afternoon for the last two, and the tech crews had the time around and in between and all through dinner. Three rehearsal hours were left for the evening, which was the technical dress rehearsal, where all the actors would be wearing full costume for the first time and all the tech cues would be run, too.

Just as everybody was gathering for dinner, George sniping at Toni for having brought dinner from KFC instead of making someone cook something a human could actually eat, Julia, with Tad and Hamlet trailing behind, burst into the kitchen, waving an envelope over her head.

"Guess who's coming to the opening!" she said, her voice half an octave higher than normal. "The governor!"

Cheers went up around the kitchen, Hamlet started barking, and Kent began stamping his feet. Everybody joined him, and the floor shook so that glasses began to rattle in the cupboards.

"And that's not all!" Julia said when the racket had died down. "Perry's office called this afternoon. Congressman Perry—the one who just announced he's running for governor next year. He'd already declined the invitation we sent, but they apparently got wind of the governor's plans and decided they didn't want to be left out."

"Didn't he jump on the 'dump arts funding' bandwagon last winter?" George asked.

Julia beamed. "That was before he declared for governor. Obviously, the Addison Opera House is already the in place to be."

"The mayor, the governor, a congressman," Del said. "So what's with the senators?"

Julia tossed the envelope onto the table. "We tried. You can't have everything."

"We'll have dueling limos," George said. "I'll bet as soon as the mayor finds out the governor's coming, even he'll turn up in a stretch."

"And that's not all," Julia said. "Three more caterers signed on this afternoon to bring goodies to the reception afterward, and a vineyard up north has donated all the champagne—excuse me, premium Michigan sparkling wine—we can use. Plus, reviewers are coming from Detroit, Toledo, and Cleveland, and..." She paused for dramatic effect as Joan came in.

"What did I miss?" Joan asked.

"And *Time* magazine's doing a feature on Shakespeare festivals across the country. Since we're the newest and since the writer they're sending usually does TV and movies, he knows Phillip, and he's planning to make our company his lead!"

"Not too much pressure," Toni said. "Just your average opening night."

Joan patted Toni on the back. "Fear not, my dear. We're doing *Richard*, after all—and we have our ghost! Why do you think all this is happening? I've told you and told you—ghosts bring good luck."

That night, though, it didn't look as if Marsden or anything else could save us from disaster. The rehearsal was chaos. People missed their cues because they couldn't make costume changes fast enough. The computer glitch that was supposed to have been fixed wasn't, and lights kept going up and down on their own, leaving actors in the darkness and lighting up empty bits of the stage. Toni, up in the booth with the demented light board, was so traumatized that she burst into tears and the whole show came to a stop. Even though she wasn't on mike, we could hear her sobs all the way down on the stage.

By the time I went onstage, I was so nervous I was sweating through my costume. It was a miracle I could remember a single word I was supposed to say. The lights onstage seemed too bright and the theatre was a dark gaping hole, like a mouth, waiting to swallow me. I tripped twice because the pant legs of my costume were too long and my boot heels kept catching on them. I wasn't the crown prince; I was Jared Kingsley, doing something I'd never wanted to do, didn't know how to do, and never wanted to do again as long as I lived. Tad, on the other hand, played our scene as if everything was going perfectly. No sweating, no shaking, no forgetting lines. For the first time, I understood what it meant that Tad was a pro.

We might as well have skipped the smothering altogether. The lights at the front of the stage came up instead of the ones on us, so the only thing that could be seen from the audience during the scene was the outside of the big rock termite hill. And when Kent had left, when the lights were supposed to come up on Richard on the stage below, that's when they came up on our platform, just as we were untangling ourselves from the covers and climbing out of the bed. "Oh, fine!" Phillip said. "The princes rise from the dead to take back the throne and the story of Richard the Third is lost forever."

"Don't worry about it," George said to Toni as she drove the van home afterward, muttering under her breath. "There's still final dress and preview. Plenty of time to clean it all up." Then he turned around to look at Joan, who was sitting next to me in the backseat, knitting away in the dark, humming gently to herself. "We don't need a ghost; we need a computer nerd!" Joan didn't stop knitting or humming, either one.

❖ ❖ ❖

Tuesday night was final dress—costumes and make-up. Tad's and my dressing room had been cleaned up and a new mirror put up at his place. It was a nice ordinary rectangular mirror, without streaks and pits, and I wished they'd given me one to match. The whole time I was putting on my makeup, doing my best to ignore Tad's predictions that I would fall on my face and make a fool of myself, I kept imagining that face again, hovering just above my own, its dark eyes spaces glaring at me. I kept feeling the old dampness, smelling the old smell. Tad rattled on about how bad I would look, how I'd probably never be allowed in another show, and I found myself positively hating him. It was only the memory of my plan—the trick I would play on him opening night in front of the governor, the mayor, the congress-man, and the writer from *Time* magazine—that kept me going.

Not one awful thing happened at final dress. The computer really had been fixed this time, the lights and sound worked perfectly, and I began to feel just the littlest bit like the crown prince again. The costume, which had been rehemmed, helped. It wasn't all that different from the other men's costumes, but the gold buttons and crown insignia and the extra piping along the edges of the tunic and the high collar were just enough to give it a regal look. I checked it in the full-length mirror in the men's dressing room and found myself automatically standing straighter, throwing back my shoulders. And once I was onstage, the lights didn't seem quite so dazzling or the darkness so threatening.

Afterward, as everybody was congratulating everybody else for a good job, I reminded myself not to get cocky. There hadn't been an audience yet. There would be an audience for the first time the next night. Not many—the volunteers who'd been working on publicity, the tech people who didn't have to work the show, the ushers, and a lot of people from the college who'd been invited for free—but an audience.

"Nothing to it," Marsden said when I told him how nervous I was. "Acting is in your blood and your bones. You'll see. Knowing the audience is there, listening to them breathe and shift in their seats, feeling their attention—and you will feel their attention, as powerful as the lights on your face—will bring you up to the mark. You'll give the best performance of your life. This is the beginning of your career, my boy!"

Career. It didn't seem possible. "Tad says when the audience is there—"

Marsden pounded the checkerboard with a fist, so that the checkers jumped. "Tad! The boy has all the sensitivity of a slug. He does what he has been trained to do, raised to do. And feels nothing. *Feels nothing!* Radiates nothing." He twiddled his mustache. "I will come to the preview performance. I will sit in the balcony, where no one will sense my presence. But you'll know I'm there. And you'll see—the audience will make you better. For a real actor, it always does."

It happened just the way he'd said it would. It helped, knowing he was out there in the darkness. And I did feel the audience. Even so, even though it was me, Jared, aware of them, I somehow felt more like the prince than ever.

And then it was over. The next time we did the play, it would be opening night. Phillip dismissed everyone as soon as they were out of costume. "Notes tomorrow afternoon and a line run. Nothing else. I want everyone to rest. Your bodies and minds and voices are your instruments, so take care of them. Each of you needs all the energy you can muster on this stage tomorrow night. So rest. Take care of yourselves. Tomorrow afternoon in the rehearsal hall at two."

That night, I slept in our room. I dreamed about limousines crashing into each other, skidding into the front of the opera house, and exploding in a ball of flame. I dreamed about audiences, thousands and thousands of faces, leering at me. I dreamed I was standing onstage with no clothes on. Rest, Phillip had said! Every time I woke up, sweating and panting from one nightmare, I went back and had another, worse one.

CHAPTER
TWENTY-THREE

The limousines had come and they had not, of course, crashed into each other or exploded the opera house. Before the house was open for people to take their seats, I sneaked up the aisle and peeked into the lobby. The governor, the congressman, and the mayor were there with their wives, surrounded by people whispering to each other, trying to stare without seeming to. The politicians were all smiling, a little stiffly, I thought, and talking at each other as they looked at the display of posters and programs I'd created. Marsden's picture was right there in the center. He, too, has an audience tonight, I thought. He would like that.

At Tad's and my places in the dressing room, there were roses in pop bottles, both white, the color of the house of York. A card with my name on it leaned against mine. It was from Phillip and Julia. "Here's to a fine and memorable debut," it said in Julia's elegant handwriting. "May it be only the beginning. Break a leg!" I held the card for a moment, running my finger over the words. A beginning. I hoped so.

Tad, in his underwear, was putting on his make-up already. He ignored me, and I went to get my costume from the rack, ignoring him, too.

As I took the hanger down, I heard a crash. "Oops," he said. I turned around, to see my rose lying on the counter in a puddle of water that was slowly spreading across the writing on the card, wiping it out. "Sorry." His voice was mocking. "How clumsy of me!"

I felt my fingers tighten on the shoulder of my costume, but I didn't say anything. I didn't even move to clean it up, just shrugged and watched the water pool around my makeup box and then drip over the edge of the counter. In my shorts pocket was the message from Phillip I would leave for Kent—my revenge against Tad. It told him to change the smothering scene the way Marsden and I had worked out, assuring him that Tad and I would change places in the bed. I had typed it in the business office and practiced the way Phillip initialed memos on the company bulletin board, until even I couldn't have told which was real and which was a copy. When the play began, I would tape the message to Kent's mirror, where he'd be sure to see it when he changed costumes from monk, which he played in the second scene, to murderer.

I had just put my costume on when Toni knocked at the dressing room door and stuck her head in. "Phone call for you, Jared. You can take it up in the office."

I hurried upstairs and picked up the phone in the empty room. "Hello?"

"If it doesn't sound too weird coming from a half-paralyzed old geezer in a wheelchair, break a leg!"

I had to swallow around a sudden lump in my throat to answer. "Hi, Pop. It's not too weird."

"You ready for opening night?"

Was I? "As ready as I can be, I guess."

"You'll be fine. Wish I could be there to see the show."

"There'll be others," I said, and knew that one way or another, that was true. "It's just the beginning."

"How about that! You're starting to sound like your mother."

"Would you mind having two actors in the family?"

"Mind? I'd be proud."

"So how're *you* doing?" I asked.

"Oh, you know me—I'm getting on with it." Pop put on his stand-up comic voice. "You should see me move my little finger! Sam, my physical terrorist, says I'll be playing the violin again in no time."

"You never played the violin in your life," I said.

"Don't tell Sam; it'll discourage him." There was a pause and I could hear the music they piped into the nursing home lobby in the background. When Pop spoke again, his voice had changed. "It's not going too fast, guy. So you hang in there, okay?"

"Okay. You hang in there, too." I had a pretty good idea what he was trying to tell me. What in some part of me I'd known all along. I might not be going to live with Pop ever again.

"Sure thing," he said. "We're both survivors. You remember that."

"I will."

When we'd said good-bye, I went to stand back-stage. I would survive, all right. But I was going to be more than a survivor. A whole lot more.

The audience was coming in now to take their seats, the sound of their talking and laughter filling the theatre. I concentrated on that. Very, very soon, the show would begin. My stomach was churning, my hands sweating at the thought, but it wasn't all nervousness now. Part of it was excitement. This wasn't only a beginning for me. It was the first performance of the first show of the first season of a brand-new theatre company—a company that promised to be so important, even the governor of the state wanted to be there for its birth. There was a feeling of celebration in the air. "It's going to work," Toni had said on the way over in the van, and everyone had agreed—even George.

If the audience had been good for the show last night, how much better this much bigger one with its reviewers and celebrities ought to be. I hoped Marsden was out there watching—from the balcony maybe, which was closed to the public. And I hoped Joan was right. I hoped just having a theatre ghost meant good luck. Suddenly, the houselights dimmed and the music began. I caught my breath and waited as the audience got quiet. Even backstage, I could feel their attention beginning to focus on the stage. Then the lights went out on the audience and up on Richard.

"Now is the winter of our discontent made glorious summer by this son of York...."

I stayed there, listening through the whole first scene, then slipped away to leave the message for Kent.

My scene was at the beginning of act 3. As act 2 ended, I went to my place and stood out of sight at the back of the center platform, waiting for the trumpets that signaled my entrance. When they sounded, I took a deep breath and walked out into the light.

Almost before I knew it, it was over. "But come, my lord, and with a heavy heart, thinking on them, go I unto the Tower," I said, and followed Tad and his guard offstage.

"Good work," I heard someone whisper as I headed for the dressing room. Had it been good? I wondered. After all the rehearsal, all the nerves, I had no memory of the scene at all. "Memorable debut," Phillip and Julia's card had said. I hoped somebody would remember it—all that was left of it for me was the feel of the lights and an echo of my voice saying my final line.

I don't know where Tad went afterward, except that he didn't come to the dressing room with me. It was empty when I went in. Empty, damp, and cold. I shivered. The odor was back, as strong as it had ever been.

As I turned to leave, I noticed that my rose was back in its bottle, the bottle full of water. My make-up box had been moved. In its place, next to the rose in front of my mirror, was Marsden's scrapbook, the one that had disappeared the day I first saw him. The one I'd never had a chance to finish looking at. On top was a note written in spidery handwriting. "For the next great actor of the American stage, on the occasion of his debut performance." I grinned. He was overdoing it a little, but what the heck. At least I'd survived my first scene.

I closed the door, sat down at my place, and opened the book to the first page, the photograph of Marsden as a young man.

A few minutes later, I'd come to the empty pages at the back. I leafed through them then, checking to be sure there was nothing more, and came to the last page, one of the double ones with an oval cut out for a photograph. The oval was empty. As I turned the page, I felt something in the bottom corner, as if something had slipped down between the two leaves of the page. I reached in and pulled out a wad of newspaper clippings, folded small, crumbling at the edges. Gently, trying to keep from tearing the brittle paper, I unfolded them.

Moments later, I looked up from reading a review. The odor in the room was stronger than ever and I saw again the shadowy face, the eyes, the smudge of mouth hovering above my own reflection in the mirror. The review had been written in Chicago the year before Marsden's appearance in Addison. I read the last part of it again. "Last night found Mr. Marsden in a hilarious state of inebriety. Unfortunately, the play was not a comedy. One would never have known it listening to the laughter emanating from the galleries. Perhaps someone in this city recommended liquor for the gentleman's 'cold.' If Mr. Marsden expects to retain his hold on the popular heart, he will avoid the too-frequent publication of such items as this."

Inebriety. I didn't know the word, but "liquor for the gentleman's 'cold'" made it easy to guess the meaning. Marsden had been drunk onstage. I scanned the next few crumbling reviews. The tone had changed. There were no more references to the great American tragedian. Some were mixed; some were downright mean. Finally, I came to one from the *Addison Gazette*. It was the review of the opening-night performance of *The Lost Is Found* here at the Addison Opera House. "Mr. Marsden last starred in this city as Macbeth in Shakespeare's historical play of that name, with more or less success. In that part, however poorly played, the spectator could still look upon him with a feeling of respect for his name, so honored in the annals of the western stage. We regret to say that Mr. Marsden, in his current role, inspires only feelings of sadness."

The cold and smell intensified and I looked up. The face was still there in the mirror. As I watched, shivering and gasping for breath, the image sharpened. The smudges became eyes; the dark line that could have been a mouth became a mustache. And then Marsden was fully there, his hat cocked, his tie snugged against his high white collar, and his eyes burning with furious intensity. The face in the mirror had been Marsden all along, I realized. It was the same Marsden I had seen for just a moment, sneering and glaring, the first time I watched him appear. The ghost George had warned us about.

"I'd forgotten those were in there," he said. "Those reviewers were fools. All fools. Country bumpkins. None of them would have known Edmund Kean from a circus barker had they not been told by the New York critics what to say."

I looked away, frightened by the look in his eyes. The last clipping was another from the *Addison Gazette*. It had been torn in half. I spread the pieces on the back page of the scrapbook, holding their torn edges together. GARRICK MARSDEN REPLACED IN *THE LOST IS FOUND* was the headline. Edward

Anderson, the manager of the touring company, had announced that a last-minute replacement, a teacher at the local college, would take the role previously played by Mr. Marsden.

"You lied to me," I said.

Marsden brushed past me, leaving a chill in the air as he moved, and leaned on the counter. "What is truth?"

"The truth is, you were a drunk."

"I played the finest theatres in New York and London. I played the great tragic roles. All of them. Hamlet, Macbeth. Richard! I was a great actor. That, Jared Kingsley, is also truth."

"What really happened here? Your coming to this town was no good deed. Your reviews had been terrible for months."

Marsden sneered. "Good deed! *A good deed* is what Edward said he was doing when he gave me the role. And then, because of some idiot country reviewer, some cretin scribbler from the *Addison Gazette*, he had the colossal effrontery to replace me—Garrick Marsden—with an amateur!"

"How did you really die?"

Marsden shook his head. "An irony of timing. I was struck, as I told you, by a falling sandbag. A sandbag meant for another."

"Meant?"

"Of course meant. You don't suppose I was going to slink away like some whipped dog! Edward gave me a minor role when he took away the lead, but I saw what he intended to do. When the run of the show was over, I would have been out of the company. Left on my own in the provinces without so much as train fare to New York. This"—he swept his arm in a half circle—"this wretched little room, was the dressing room I was given. It wasn't even mine. I had to share it with the supernumeraries, what you call 'the warm bodies.' Me, in here! I had had the star dressing room at the Theatre Royal, and they put me in *here*!"

He paused, and I was aware of the music coming from the stage. "It was a simple plan, really. I bribed a stagehand with a bottle of fine whiskey to set a sandbag where it would fall when a drop curtain was raised. It was to fall on the chair where my replacement would be sitting at the end of the first scene. Except that that amateur, that...*professor*...confused his blocking. We were the only two on the stage and he took the wrong chair, leaving me no choice but to sit in the other. If I had done otherwise, it would have seemed to the audience that *I* had made some sort of blunder. I intended to move before the scene changed, of course, but he jumped his cue and ended the scene four speeches early. It was all over before I had a chance to react."

"You meant to murder your replacement."

"It would have been an accident, of course. Tragic, but an accident. Falling sandbag. Such things happened. And there would have been no one, then, but me to take over the role."

I thought of all the time I had spent in the Trap Room, listening to Marsden's stories, taking his advice, playing checkers. All the time, I had believed him as he played the kindly, funny old theatre ghost. I had believed him. Every minute, I'd believed him! "How could you do such a thing?"

He smiled then, and I felt a chill run all the way up my spine. "It's not so unusual, is it? Removing an obstacle—that's all I was doing. As Richard did with the princes. You yourself would do it if you could."

I shook my head. "Never."

He leaned close, his eyes boring into mine, and I shuddered. "Can you honestly tell me you haven't wished to be the only son, the only heir to the Kingsley name? Do you mean to tell me you have never wished Tad simply out of the way?"

I pushed the memory of my dream—me taking a bow between Phillip and Julia—as far away as I could. It had been a dream, that's all, like the crashing limousines. I had no control over my dreams. "You lied about the fencing match, too," I said. "Didn't you? You meant to get Tad out of the way then."

Marsden toyed with his watch chain. "I wouldn't call what I've done lying. I am an actor. I have been playing a role. Brilliantly, I might add."

He pushed himself to his feet and stood over me as I cowered back in my chair. "I was the finest actor of my time," he said. "Of any time. I've proved it once again. You believed me. Everyone believed me.

194

The friendly old theatre ghost, taking care of the opera house, looking out for his fellow actors." He laughed. "I haven't lost my touch."

"George didn't believe you," I said.

"Until I saved Tad's life." Marsden laughed again, and the tone of it set my teeth on edge. "And to think that was only a mistake."

"A mistake?"

"I thought I had finished him off with the curtains. Resilient boy! Ah well, that will all change tonight, and I'll have my way."

"Your way?"

The look Marsden gave me then stopped my breath. "That simpleton playing Richard's mother, that English woman, thinks I am here to bring this company—and this theatre—good luck. What possible reason could I have for wishing this godforsaken place, or any actors still alive to tread the boards, still able to perform Shakespeare for a living audience, *luck*? Why should I want for others what I have lost so irretrievably for myself? I may have failed with the fencing match. I may have failed again with the fire. But tonight, I will not fail. Tonight, before the curtain falls on opening night, a death will close the New World Shakespeare Company forever."

"Whose death?" I asked, though I was all too sure I knew the answer.

"You know. You planned it. And you've already set it in motion."

My mouth and throat were so dry, my tongue stuck to the roof of my mouth as I tried to speak. "But that's nothing but a prank. A trick. It can't *kill* him!"

"You think not?" He began to pace the length of the counter. "After all our time together, all we've meant to each other, I'm surprised at you. This is what you've wanted from the moment you heard the sound of applause. To be the crown prince. The successor to the throne. Here I am, ready to help, and you tell me you haven't been counting on that all along? Gloucester and Buckingham we have been—"

"Help? Help? I don't want you to do anything. I just wanted to scare him, that's all. It's nothing but a prank!"

"Oh, he'll be scared. First he'll be scared—"

"I don't want you to do anything!" I said again, my voice cracking.

Marsden stopped directly in front of me and leaned down till his face, with its wrinkles and pouches, was so close to mine, I could feel the bristles of his mustache touch my forehead. The foul, damp, musty odor of this terrible room seemed to pour over me.

"I can smile and murder whiles I smile, and cry 'Content!' to that which grieves my heart, and wet my cheeks with artificial tears, and frame my face to all occasions.... Can I do this, and cannot get a crown? Tut, were it farther off, I'll pluck it down."

He smiled then and stood up. "That's Richard also. In the play before this one—*Henry the Sixth*. Richard of Gloucester—like you, like me—an actor! Like you, like me, a villain who revels in his villainy."

He reached down then and took the scrapbook out of my lap. "An hour from now, you'll have your crown and you'll have me to thank. Garrick Marsden, the finest actor of his—or *any*—time." And he was gone.

CHAPTER
TWENTY-FOUR

I hurried out of the dressing room as act 3 ended and intermission began. Phillip and Del were just coming offstage, wiping the sweat from their faces. I ducked in front of them and hurried to the Greenroom, looking for Tad. The warm bodies were there in their soldier costumes, some of them playing cards, and Joan was sitting at the end of the couch, knitting. "Has anyone seen Tad?" I asked just as George came in. He was dressed now as Richmond, the role he played in act 5.

"I saw him awhile ago heading downstairs," he said.

"It's going brilliantly, don't you think?" Joan asked him as I hurried away.

Downstairs. I plunged down the stairs into the semidarkness. There was nothing down here except the prop storage and the Trap Room. Had he come down to find a place to smoke? The overhead bulb was not on in the prop room, so I didn't bother going in. I didn't think he had the nerve to hang out among all those dusty shapes in the darkness. The Trap Room door, however, was open a crack and the light was on. I shoved the door open and went inside. He was not there in the trap space, but I smelled cigarette smoke.

Tad was sitting in Marsden's chair, a lit cigarette in one hand and a Styrofoam cup in the other. "So this is where you've been hiding out whenever you disappear," he said. "If the bulb hadn't burned out in the prop room, I might never have found this place." He pointed to the lamp on the table. "Shame on you, lighting this thing down here. Don't you know you could cause another fire? After the first one, you'd think you would learn a lesson."

I pointed to his cigarette. "How come *you* didn't?"

"I did," he said, grinning and holding up the cup. "Drop a butt in water and it can't hurt anything."

"We need to change places in the smothering scene," I said. "Kent's going to be on the other side of the bed."

Tad took a long drag on his cigarette and puffed smoke toward me. "Why would Kent be on the other side of the bed?"

"Because he got a note from Phillip to change sides."

"I was there for notes this afternoon. I didn't hear that."

"He didn't tell him then. He wrote it down—left it for him in the dressing room."

Tad shook his head. "I don't think so. Dad wouldn't ask an actor to change his blocking for the first time on opening night. Anyway, why would he want to change anything? It was working fine."

Kent would have asked the same question. In the note, I'd blamed the lighting. "Something about the lights maybe."

Tad flicked ashes into the cup. "Why didn't Dad tell me about this?"

"Because he couldn't find you! Because you're down here rotting your lungs and wrecking your voice."

Tad shook his head again. "Nice try, but it won't work."

"What won't work?"

He dropped the cigarette into the cup. "Hear that sizzle? Not so much as a spark left." He tipped the cup slowly and poured the water, ashes, and cigarette butt over the arm of the chair onto the red rug. My rug. "You're just trying to get me to change places with you so Kent'll smother me first—so I'll have to lie there pretending to be dead with that comforter over my head while he smothers you. Well, it won't work. Dad wouldn't change blocking on opening night. And he wouldn't send *you* to give me the message!"

He set the cup on the table and then, only half-pretending an accident as he stood up, knocked the table sideways, sending table, lamp, and tape player crashing to the floor. The batteries popped out of the tape player and the lamp broke. Oil spread out, soaking gradually into the rug. "Oops," Tad said, popping a piece of gum into his mouth. "Just me being clumsy again."

He went past me and out.

For a moment, just the tiniest breath of a moment, I wished I could leave the prank alone, let Marsden do whatever it was he had planned. But it wasn't any more than that—a wish. Like the dream, it didn't mean anything. I looked at the mess on the floor. It didn't matter, I realized. My hideout was already ruined. Not by Tad, by Marsden. I didn't want to come down here ever again.

In the Greenroom, I looked for Kent. He wasn't there. Tad was leaning over one of the warm bodies, looking at the cards in his hand. I tried the men's dressing room. Kent wasn't there, either. I wanted to find him before intermission was over, before the fourth act started. Once it did, there was only one scene before Richard gave Tyrrel the order to kill the princes; and only moments later, the audience was to see him do it. I tried the Greenroom again. And then I heard the music that meant the inter-mission was over.

Julia and Joan went past me on their way to the stage. Moments later, the act began. I went backstage, staying between the platforms and the back-drop, where I couldn't be seen, and crossed to see if Kent was already stage right, waiting for his entrance. He wasn't.

"Come, madam," I heard from the stage, "you must straight to Westminster, there to be crowned Richard's royal queen."

The first scene was nearly halfway through.

I hurried back and checked the men's dressing room again. Just as I was about to give up, Kent came out of the bathroom, fastening his costume. I practically threw myself at him and grabbed his arm. "Phillip's changed his mind," I said. "We're supposed to do the smothering scene the way we've always done it."

Kent shrugged. "Okay. I wondered why he wanted to change it—seemed fine to me." He checked himself in the mirror. "Better get to your place."

I took a breath so deep, it seemed to come clear from my toes. Everything would be all right. Kent would smother me first, only pretend to smother Tad, and leave. There would never be anything except the sheet over Tad's face, and that wouldn't even scare him, much less kill him. Maybe Marsden had been lying anyway. It's what he was, after all. Not an actor—a liar. A drunk and a liar. Probably he'd never had a way to make that prank into something dangerous anyway. He was just trying to scare me. Just trying to make me think I was like him. Like Richard. Well, I wasn't.

I climbed the stairs toward the Tower platform and stopped behind Tad. Everything was going to be all right.

Kent was onstage now. "Dar'st thou resolve to kill a friend of mine?" Phillip asked.

"Aye my Lord, but I had rather kill two enemies," Kent answered.

"Why, there thou hast it! Two deep enemies..."

That was our cue. Tad went up the last two steps and onto the platform. I followed. He got into the bed, I got in after him, and we pulled the sheet up over our heads. "You didn't really think I'd fall for it, did you?" Tad whispered as he turned on his side. I turned, too, ignoring the jab he gave me with his elbow before we settled into the stillness of sleep the audience would see when the lights came up.

Now Buckingham was asking Richard for what Richard had promised him in return for doing his dirty work. Richard was putting him off. "Thou troublest me," Phillip said as he moved away. "I am not in the vein." Everyone except Buckingham left the stage.

Del's voice rose. "Is it even so? Rewards he my true service with such deep contempt? Made I him king for this?" The end-of-scene music crept in beneath his voice. "O, let me think on Hastings, and be gone to Brecknock while my fearful head is on!"

The lights faded out onstage and, after a moment, came up on our platform. The music got louder, and I felt the platform vibrate as Kent came up the steps and stood next to the bed. *Fooled you*, I thought, directing it to Marsden, wherever he was.

The scene went as it always had. Tad managed to kick me twice while he struggled as Kent held the comforter against his chin, and I managed to keep from reacting. He settled into stillness again and Kent stood up. I felt the muscles in my shoulders relax. It was all over.

But before Kent began to move away from the bed, I felt the cold—felt the air sucked from my lungs. And then, as I used every ounce of will I could muster not to move, I felt the comforter and sheet over my face slip sideways and the lights glared against my tightly closed eyes as the weight of Marsden settled onto me, holding me down. Tad moaned a tiny, muffled moan and I felt him stiffen next to me. I squinted against the light. Marsden was not fully there, but I could see that blurring of the air above me, could feel him straddling Tad's and my bodies with a knee on either side, holding the comforter tightly against Tad's face. I tried to move, but I was pinned firmly in place, my arms at my sides. Kent was standing, looking down at the princes' bodies. Kent couldn't see Marsden, I realized. Kent never had. He didn't know what was happening.

Tad moaned again and the sound was suddenly cut off. I could feel Tad's arms twitching against mine. My mind raced. How long did it take to smother someone? What could I do to make Marsden let go? And then I remembered the trick Marsden had played on that actor he wanted to get rid of. "There's nothing so ghastly as the feel of an audience that knows something is going wrong," he'd said. "Even ghastlier is the moment when you know that *they* know that whatever's wrong, it's your fault."

"They can see you," I whispered up at him. "The audience can see you. And you look like a fool, dressed like that. They know something's wrong—they know you don't belong."

I felt Marsden's weight shift. I imagined him looking over his shoulder, out toward the audience.

"Some great actor," I whispered as the music's volume rose again and Kent began moving toward the steps. "Coming into someone else's scene like this. They'll think you're drunk again. They'll laugh at you. Can't you feel the audience starting to laugh at you?"

The weight shifted again, but Marsden hadn't let up on Tad. I could see the comforter still jammed against Tad's face, feel Tad's legs beginning to twitch. Kent was moving down the stairs.

"You've been forgotten, you know," I whispered. "Nobody even remembers your name." Tad's body had been rigid against me. Now, I felt it slump. Desperately, I went on. "But they'll remember tonight. Not Garrick Marsden, great actor. They'll remember Garrick Marsden, fool. Garrick Marsden, drunk. I'm not like you. I wouldn't be like you for anything in the world. I'm embarrassed even to know you."

With a tremendous bang, a light exploded overhead, showering sparks down on us. I heard a gasp from the audience and another light went, and another, plunging the platform into darkness. The weight vanished, and I sat up, flinging the comforter to the floor as I gasped for breath in the icy cold. Tad lay unmoving in the darkness. The music swelled as Toni bumped the volume to cover the confusion, trying to make it all seem intended. I felt Tad's neck, looking for a pulse. "Kent," I called, as loud as I dared, and realized he was too far away to hear me. He was to come on stage left as soon as the lights for the next scene came up. There was a faint movement under my fingers on Tad's neck. A pulse. He wasn't dead!

I pulled him to a sitting position, and he opened his eyes as the lights came on at the front of the stage.

Phillip's voice came through the scrim that kept us from being seen by the audience. "Kind Tyrrel, am I happy in thy news?"

"If to have done the thing you gave in charge beget your happiness, be happy then, for it is done, my lord."

I helped Tad to the edge of the bed and let him lean on me as we crept down the stairs and offstage behind the platforms. *It is* not *done!* I thought at the vanished Marsden. *You failed again!*

CHAPTER TWENTY-FIVE

Tad hadn't seen the ghost, but he didn't need to see him to know what was happening when Marsden tried to smother him. I took Tad straight to our dressing room. He was still leaning on me, still shaking so hard, he could hardly walk. When I opened the door to the dressing room, we both gasped in surprise. It was trashed. Completely trashed. The mirrors were broken, the chairs overturned, the clothes racks tipped onto the floor. Our clothes and makeup had been thrown every which way. The pop bottles that had held the roses were shattered and the roses torn apart, petals strewn over the wreckage.

"I think they'd better board this place up again," I said. "Like George said."

Tad stood for a moment, looking at the slivers of

the old round mirror. "That was really the ghost, that face in the mirror, wasn't it?"

I nodded.

"I didn't think mirrors could reflect ghosts."

"I think that's vampires," I said. What I was thinking was that it was weird—the old mirrors in here had always reflected the *real* Marsden, the one I couldn't see. "I don't think people know all that much about ghosts. Phillip called them 'disembodied.' He said they couldn't hurt you."

Tad rubbed his face and shook his head. "Dad was wrong!"

We went to the Greenroom then and sat on the couch, not doing anything, not saying anything, till the warm bodies went off to get ready for the battle scenes at the end of the show. Then Tad turned to me. "The ghost was there during our fencing match, wasn't he? That's why I couldn't hit you."

I shrugged. "Could be."

"And it was the ghost who pulled the tip off your foil."

I shrugged again. "I only know I didn't."

"I don't understand why he saved me in the fire and then tried to smother me tonight."

"Who can tell what a ghost is thinking," I said.

"Do you suppose he's still here somewhere?"

"I think he's gone. Permanently." I didn't know whether I believed that or whether I just wanted to believe it.

Tad shuddered. "He'd better be." We just sat

then, both of us taking long, slow breaths as we listened to the progress of the play through the Greenroom speakers.

"Now civil wounds are stopped, peace lives again: That she may long live here, God say amen!" As the music swelled after the play's final line, the audience burst into applause.

"Let's go," I said. "Curtain call."

When Phillip had blocked the curtain call, he had wanted Tad and me to come out and take our bow holding hands. Tad had refused. But when it was time to go out onto the stage, he grabbed for my hand. I started to pull away, but then I changed my mind. He was still, after all this time, shaking. Just this once, I told myself.

The audience was on its feet, some of them with their hands clapping over their heads. I knew none of that was for me or for Tad—our parts were too small for anyone to take any special notice of us. But it was wonderful anyway. It felt like warm waves coming up onto the stage and breaking over us all. When Phillip came out, last, there were whistles and shouts of "Bravo!" and it seemed forever before we all locked hands, bowed one last time, and then turned to file offstage on either side, leaving Phillip to take his final bow alone.

When everyone had gathered in the Greenroom, we told them the story of Tad's near miss and the ghost's treachery. Marsden hadn't actually been seen by anyone but me. All that the others knew was that the Tower lights had suddenly blown out. But it didn't take much effort from Tad to convince them about the evil ghost. Even Joan shook her head and clucked her tongue and patted Tad's shoulder when he'd finished telling about it.

No one had ever known that Marsden and I had been friends. No one thought now—not even Tad—that I might have had anything to do with what happened. And Kent never mentioned the note. Even if he had, I'm not sure that anybody would have blamed me for anything. I'd become a kind of hero now, for saving Tad from the ghost.

"I told you so!" George said when everyone had inspected the wreckage of the little dressing room. "I said it should have been left boarded up all along."

"I think we'll close it up now," Phillip said.

"Do you suppose he's really gone?" Laurence asked.

"He'd better be," Toni said. "We can't afford to keep replacing lights!"

Julia put an arm around Tad and pulled him to her. "We can't afford to replace princes, either!"

When the audience went out through the lobby, they found the display of historical posters and programs destroyed, the bulletin board broken in half. The bill for *The Lost Is Found*, staring Garrick Marsden, was missing entirely.

Nobody ever knew whether the governor really liked the play or only thought he should like it, but he wrote a letter to the editor of *Time* magazine complaining when the writer said that *Richard III* as an installment of the *Star Wars* saga didn't really work. "The New World Shakespeare Company of Addison, Michigan," the governor's letter said, "is the newest cultural jewel in our state's crown, and I, for one, thought the production a great success."

Time was the only negative voice—all the other reviews were raves—and since the article didn't even appear till *Richard* was over, it didn't do any harm; by the second day after the opening, all three weekends had sold out. Rehearsals for *The Taming of the Shrew* started the next Monday, and Tad and I were given the roles of two of the servants. Both of us had some good, funny lines.

The little dressing room was closed and padlocked shut. "Even though the ghost is gone," Julia said, "it's better not to use that place. There's something unpleasant there—something that gets into you somehow." Tad began bringing Hamlet to the theatre again, having decided that "just a dog" might know something about ghosts after all. Hamlet was fine everywhere else in the building, but he still growled and refused to go near the little dressing room, even with the padlock on.

Nearly being smothered by a ghost didn't change Tad at all. He was still as spoiled and obnoxious as ever. But he did stop pouring water on my futon, and Kent's extra helmet turned up one day, strapped to his motorcycle where it had been before. Kent and Laurence both told me some stories about their brothers that made me think Tad and I weren't all that different from anybody else. Even if you shared a father *and* a mother, even if you grew up with your brother, it didn't mean you were going to like him. It didn't mean he couldn't be a creep.

If I'd ever expected Phillip to be a doting father, I was out of luck. The truth was, he was a lot like Serena. What he really cared about was theatre. That was true about Julia, too. It was possible, I realized, that I'd had more real parenting from Pop than Tad had had living with both his parents all his life. When it came right down to it, what all of the Kingsleys really cared about was the theatre. If we were going to be a family, we'd just have to make do with that.

As for Marsden, I don't know. Somebody from the college said there used to be stories about a malicious ghost at the opera house, but once the movies pushed vaudeville out, the stories faded away. Maybe he really had just holed up in that dressing room for all those years, nursing his misery. And then the New World Shakespeare Company came along—bringing theatre back into his world. He'd said I called him. But it wasn't me. George had seen him before I ever came. Maybe it was doing *Richard*, the play about a man who killed anybody who got in his way. Just like he'd tried to do—and failed. And then there was Tad and me. Competition. A chance to do for me what he hadn't been able to do for himself.

Whatever Marsden wanted, he didn't get it. All he did was fail all over again. So was he back hiding out in the little dressing room, nursing the same old bitterness? A padlock can keep actors out of a nasty little room, but it can't keep a ghost in. Will he come out and try again someday? *Something* keeps Hamlet away from that door.

What's weirdest of all, maybe, is that I miss him. Or at least I miss who I thought he was. The character he played. Phillip says that the way to make an audience believe your character is to find a piece of him inside yourself. So I've been thinking—in Garrick Marsden, the evil actor bent on revenge, didn't there have to be a bit of the kindly old caretaker? Isn't that bit what I believed in when we played checkers, when he told me his stories and made me laugh and convinced me I could be an actor someday? And didn't he really like me? At least a little?

There's another story about the opening that people don't much talk about, but I can't get it out of my mind. After the excitement of the opening-night party, we had a day off before the second night's performance. So on June thirtieth, nobody went to the Addison Opera House till nearly seven o'clock in the evening. That's when Phyllis went into the costume shop and found one of the irons turned on, sitting on a badly scorched ironing board, its cord nearly melted. It was unplugged. Phyllis says she was in a hurry to press the dress Julia wore to the party, and she doesn't remember turning the iron off afterward. Nobody knows how the iron got unplugged. Nobody knows.

Even though I still do my best to stay away from Tad, I don't go down to the Trap Room anymore; I've taken to hanging out in the Greenroom mostly. It turns out Laurence likes chess, so we keep a board set up there. And in between stage combat classes, Kent's been working with me on fencing. One of these days, I'm going to beat Tad for real.

I don't know if Pop's going to get better so that I can go live with him again. But I keep in mind what he's always told me. *The only thing that matters is how you play 'em.* I figure I'm playing my cards about as well as I know how, and I can't do any better than that.